The Seagull Who Was Afraid To Fly

By
Steven P. Wickstrom

PublishAmerica
Baltimore

© 2004 by Steven P. Wickstrom

All rights reserved. No part of this book may be reproduced, stored in a retrieval system or transmitted in any form or by any means without the prior written permission of the publishers, except by a reviewer who may quote brief passages in a review to be printed in a newspaper, magazine or journal.

First printing

ISBN: 1-4137-1890-6
PUBLISHED BY PUBLISHAMERICA, LLLP
www.publishamerica.com
Baltimore

Printed in the United States of America

The Seagull Who Was Afraid To Fly

Chapter One

"Mama," chirped Erin. "The egg is beginning to hatch."

Mama Seagull, who was sitting on the edge of the nest, looked down and watched the quivering egg. The Seagull's nest was built on a ledge on a bluff. Nearby stood a lighthouse that overlooked the ocean. Three of the four eggs that Mama Seagull laid had already hatched. There was only one to go, and it lay quivering at the bottom of the nest.

Erin had hatched out of her egg first. She was very proud of the fact that she was the firstborn. It gave her a feeling of superiority. Burt had hatched the next day, and Cal hatched a day later. Now, two days after Cal had hatched, the final egg was hatching. Papa Seagull returned just then with tidbits of fish which the young seagulls quickly devoured. He sat on the edge of the nest, next to Mama Seagull, and watched the egg start to break open.

A tiny beak broke through the top of the egg as everyone watched and waited. Soon little cracks appeared as the tiny bird started to push his way out of the confining shell. Suddenly, the top of the egg split open and a little head pushed its way out. The egg fell over and the small bird pulled itself out of the restraining shell. The tiny bird opened its mouth and wailed pitifully.

"What's the matter with him?" asked Burt as he looked up at Mama.

"He's just hungry, dear," said Mama Seagull, who put a small piece of food into the newborn's mouth.

In the process of eating, the little seagull fell over onto his side. His body, which was still moist from being inside the egg, became covered with the soft small downy feathers that were lining the nest. He pushed himself back into an upright position and sneezed.

"He looks like a little dust ball," said Burt.

"He's a dust ball with wings," laughed Erin.

"Can we keep him, Mama?" asked Cal.

"Of course we're going to keep him, dear," Mama Seagull lovingly responded. "He is your brother, after all." She then looked up at Papa Seagull. "I think that perhaps we should name him Dusty."

"Dusty, Dusty," chorused Erin, Burt, and Cal.

"It's a good name for him," laughed Papa Seagull. "His name will be Dusty."

Dusty peered at everyone with a quizzical expression on his face. He was hungry and simply wanted to be fed. After Mama Seagull finished feeding him, Dusty fell fast asleep. Erin, Burt, and Cal cuddled up next to him and also quickly went to sleep.

As the weeks went by, the young birds began to sleep less between feedings. The world outside their nest fascinated them and they would spend hours gazing up at the bluffs. The bluffs were multi- hued with earth-tone colors, including a splash of gray here and there. The colors fascinated the little seagulls and they loved watching the shadows move across the face of the cliff as the sun moved across the sky.

Mealtimes were still their favorite part of the day. They were peering over the edge of the nest when Papa Seagull flew back with a fresh batch of food. All four of the young seagulls clamored for attention so that they might be fed first.

"My goodness!" exclaimed Papa Seagull. "You would think that these children never eat, from the noise they're making."

He gave Erin a piece of fish, which she quickly devoured. He sighed and gave a piece of fish to Burt.

"I had no idea that raising children could be so exhausting," said Papa Seagull.

"They're still growing, dear," responded Mama Seagull. "In a few months they'll be old enough to find their own food."

"The sooner they learn how to fly, the better. I vaguely seem to remember what it was like to get a full night's sleep."

"I wouldn't worry about that, dear. Children always grow up too fast. They'll be out of the nest and flying before you know it."

Since all four of the young seagulls now had full tummies, they quickly fell asleep. Mama and Papa Seagull decided to take naps, also. They preened their feathers, stepped down into the nest, and settled down to sleep. Sleep was too precious a commodity to waste. In a short period of time, the nest was filled with the soft sounds of sleeping birds.

Several weeks later, Erin thought up a new game to play while they were waiting for Mama and Papa to return with more food. It was the first time that both parents had been gone at the same time. Up until now, Mama had stayed at the nest while Papa looked for food, or Papa stayed while Mama was away. One parent was always with the children. But now, they thought that the children were old enough to be left alone for a short time. Papa left Erin in charge while they were gone.

"I have a new game for us to play," announced Erin. "I just thought it up."

"Do I have to play?" asked Burt. "I don't want to play a game."

"You have to," responded Erin. "I'm the oldest and I'm in charge. So you have to play my games."

"Papa's older than you are," stated Cal.

"Papa's not here, so I'm in charge," retorted Erin.

"I'll play a game with you," said Dusty, who was trying to be helpful.

"We're ALL going to play," said Erin as she glared at Burt.

"Ok, let's play your stupid game," said Burt. "What is it anyway?"

"It's not stupid," responded Erin. "It's a good game. I call it, 'Name That Bird.'"

Burt and Cal looked at each other and groaned.

"We're going to give names to birds?" asked Dusty.

"No, stupid," responded Erin. "We're going to name the *type* of bird that it is, not give it a name. Don't you know anything?"

"I'm not stupid," said Dusty, more to himself than anyone else. He was already quite sure that he was not going to like playing Erin's game.

"Okay, since it's my game, I get to go first," said Erin.

That was just as well, since no one else wanted to be first, anyway. They all looked out over the edge of the nest to see who was flying nearby. Erin quickly spotted a seagull. This was probably cheating, since seagulls were flying around everywhere, but since it was Erin's game, she could make up her own rules.

"There's a seagull," said Erin as she pointed at it with her wing. She was very pleased with herself. "It's your turn, Burt."

Burt looked around and saw his chance to goad Erin. "There's a hawk," said Burt, pointing way up in the sky. "A hawk is much bigger than a seagull." He turned his head and stuck his tongue out at Erin. That would teach her. He had found a hawk, while all that Erin had been able to find was a seagull.

"It's your turn Cal," said Erin. She stuck her tongue out at Burt in return. She disliked the fact that Burt had found a larger bird. She was certain that Cal would not be so lucky.

Cal looked around at the sky for a minute and then pointed. "I see an albatross," said Cal, hoping that Erin would not refute him. He knew that Erin would make fun of him if he incorrectly named a bird. It was a good thing that he didn't know that Erin was upset at him also, for finding a larger bird than she had found.

"It's not fair," pouted Erin.

"Oh you're just upset because we're finding bigger and better birds than you did. You're the one who invented this game, we're just better at it, that's all," said Burt with a sly grin. He stuck his tongue out at Erin, knowing that it would irritate her. It did.

"It's your turn Dusty," said Erin impatiently. She turned and gave Burt a scorching look.

Dusty looked around, but the only birds he saw were seagulls. Erin had already pointed out a seagull so he couldn't use that one again. He was starting to get desperate and he could see that Erin was getting impatient. He didn't want to name a bird incorrectly, because he also knew that if he did, Erin would make fun of him. Just then, a large pelican flew over the nest, just above their heads. It startled all of them.

"Look, a dragon!" exclaimed Dusty.

"That's not a dragon, you idiot," said Erin as soon as she recovered from being startled by the pelican. She looked at Dusty with a disgusted look on her face. "That's a pelican. Everybody knows that! You are *so* stupid."

Dusty was devastated. If birds could blush, he would have. As it was, he was so embarrassed that he decided not to play these games ever again. He didn't want anyone to think that he was stupid, so he decided not to participate.

"Dusty wins!" announced Burt. "His dragon is larger than any of our birds. It's certainly bigger than a *seagull*." He made a face at Erin.

Erin was furious. It was bad enough that everyone saw a larger bird than she did. But to have Burt rub it in made it even worse. She was also mad at Dusty and his dragon. Pelican, she reminded herself, pelican.

"That was not a dragon," said Erin, "it was a pelican, and you know it."

"I'm not going to play this game anymore," announced Burt.

"Me neither," said Cal, who was siding with Burt.

"This is all your fault," said Erin as she glared at Dusty.

"Oh be quiet, Erin," said Burt. "It was just a dumb girl game."

"Dumb girl game," echoed Cal, who was simply imitating Burt.

Erin ruffled her feathers and sulked. She was going to punish the boys by refusing to speak to them. That would show them! Little did she know that none of the boys, however, considered that to be punishment. It was a reward perhaps, but definitely not a punishment. It was probably just as well that they were all refusing to speak to each other. As a result, everyone was quiet when Mama and Papa returned to the nest. They quickly noticed the silence.

"Well, this is different," said Papa Seagull.

"Why is everyone so quiet?" asked Mama Seagull. For a moment, nobody spoke, they all looked down at the floor of the nest.

"We saw a dragon," said Cal.

"Dusty saw a dragon," said Erin as she glared at Cal. "The rest of us saw a pelican."

Mama and Papa Seagull glanced at each other. The look said, "We shouldn't have left them alone, yet." Papa Seagull sighed. *Dragons.*

"Tell us what happened," prompted Mama Seagull.

"Erin made us play a game while you were gone," said Burt. "None of us wanted to play, but she made us play anyway. We had to name types of birds that we saw. It was Dusty's turn when a pelican flew right over our heads. It surprised us all. It's not Dusty's fault that he thought the pelican was a dragon. Erin is just being mean because she didn't win her own game."

"Dusty doesn't know the difference between a dragon and a pelican," said Erin. "He's stupid."

Mama Seagull noticed how uncomfortable and downcast Dusty was, and asked, "Erin, do you know what a dragon looks like?"

"No, Mama," answered Erin after a minute of sullen silence.

"Then Dusty wouldn't know what a dragon looks like either, would he? So then, Dusty isn't stupid, is he?"

"No, Mama," said Erin after some hesitation.

"Now, can we all forgive each other and agree to get along together?"

"Yes, Mama," the four young seagulls slowly responded.

"Good," said Papa Seagull. "Now, if nobody is hungry, I guess I'll just have to eat all this food myself." He pretended to eat some of the food. Suddenly, everyone found their appetites again. The food was quickly devoured.

After supper, Mama and Papa Seagull were sitting on the ledge next to the nest preening their feathers. Inside the nest, Dusty stretched his wings out, then folded them back and tried to make himself comfortable. His tail feathers brushed up against Erin.

"Mom," cried Erin, "Dusty's touching me."

Papa Seagull put his head down in his wings and groaned. Mama patted him on the shoulder but didn't say anything.

Burt thought this was just grand and reached out and touched Erin.

"Mom," cried Erin again, "Burt touched me, too."

Papa Seagull tried hard not to laugh.

"You're not helping, dear," said Mama Seagull softly.

Cal took advantage of the situation and also reached out to touch Erin.

"Mom," said Erin, "Cal just touched me."

Burt, Cal, and Dusty all touched Erin simultaneously.

"Mom!" wailed Erin, "they're all touching me. Make them stop."

Papa Seagull doubled over with laughter. He was trying very hard to be as silent as he could. This actually made it worse. Mama Seagull looked at him and shook her head. She let out a heavy sigh. She stood up and peered into the nest.

Burt, Cal, and Dusty all had the look of complete innocence on their faces. That in and of itself told Mama that they were guilty.

"Make them stop touching me," said Erin in a whining voice.

"I want all of you to go to sleep, now," said Mama Seagull. "Tuck your heads into your wings and go to sleep."

She waited until they all had their heads tucked into their wings before she sat down again. Mama Seagull was satisfied; it was quiet again. Except, that is, for the muffled sound of Papa Seagull's sobbing laughter.

A week later, Dusty was lying on his back, leaning up against the sloping wall of the nest. His wings were tucked back behind his head, and his legs were sticking straight out in front of him. He was totally relaxed. It was a warm, lazy, sleepy afternoon. He was idly watching the fleecy clouds overhead as they slowly drifted across the sky. The clouds were slowly changing their shapes as they sailed with the breeze.

Dusty had been watching the clouds for quite some time because he found the changing shapes fascinating to look at. He wondered what it would be like to fly up there with the clouds. He then wondered what it would be like to walk on top of one of those clouds.

"Mama, have you ever walked on top of a cloud?" asked Dusty.

"No dear, I haven't," said Mama Seagull who was sitting up on the edge of the nest. "It's not something that I've ever thought about doing before."

"If you fell asleep on a cloud, where would you wake up?" asked Dusty.

"That depends upon which direction the wind is blowing, dear," said Mama Seagull. She smiled with amusement. Children could ask some of the most interesting questions.

"Why do the clouds change shape as they go across the sky?" asked Dusty.

"Clouds do that so that they won't get bored during their travels," said Mama Seagull. "Besides, it might be fun to be able to change your shape now and then, don't you think so, dear?"

"I think it might be fun if Erin changed into a cloud and blew away," said Burt.

"Burt," said Mama Seagull.

"Well it would," said Burt.

"Burt!" said Mama Seagull.

Erin stuck her tongue out at Bert. Cal giggled.

Dusty had never thought about the ability to change shapes. That would, however, be a lot of fun. He leaned back and continued watching the clouds. In his imagination, he began to change shapes. He noticed that one cloud was in the process of changing from a tree to a horse.

"That cloud looks like a horse," said Dusty as he pointed at the sky.

Burt and Cal looked up at the clouds with interest while Erin shook her head with disgust. Mama Seagull also looked and gazed up at the clouds. Dusty had sparked their interest and imagination.

"I see a cloud that looks like a crab," said Cal.

"And there's one that looks like a fish," added Burt. "What do you see, Erin?"

"I'm not playing Dusty's game," said Erin. "You guys don't like to play my games, so I don't like to play yours."

"Suit yourself," said Burt, "but you're missing out on a lot of fun."

"I wonder if the clouds ever have races with each other," said Dusty.

Erin snorted.

"Yeah," said Burt, "a race to see who can get across the sky the fastest."

"What kind of prize would they give the winner?" asked Cal. "Do you know, Mama?"

"Yes dear, the cloud who comes in first place gets a golden lining," answered Mama Seagull. "The second place winner gets a silver lining."

"Wow," said all three boys in awe. They immediately started looking for clouds with gold or silver linings. They were disappointed when they didn't find any, so they went back to watching the shape changes.

"Hey Erin," said Burt, "that cloud right above us looks just like a dragon, doesn't it? Or would that be a pelican? You're the expert, what do you think it looks like?"

Dusty giggled to himself. He quickly covered his face with his wing. He wanted to be careful not to let Erin see him laugh.

"Mama," complained Erin, "make him stop."

"Burt," said Mama Seagull.

"Erin is such a brat," said Burt.

"Burt!" said Mama Seagull, a little more sternly this time.

Burt wisely decided to ignore Erin and went back to looking up at the clouds. He did take some satisfaction at having been able to irritate Erin. He smiled to himself as he heard Erin ruffling her feathers.

"That was a fun game Dusty," said Burt. "I'm glad that you thought it up."

Erin ruffled her feathers some more. She wanted everyone to know that she was not impressed with Dusty's game.

Within a few months the young seagulls had grown to about one-half of their adult size. Their feathers were still gray in color and would remain that way for several more months. It wasn't until their feathers turned white that seagulls were considered to be adults. Every seagull looked forward to that occasion.

It was a sunny, breezy day, and the clouds were blowing across the sky like giant billowy marshmallows. Dusty was inside the nest watching the clouds turn into different shapes. It was his favorite game, but he usually played it by himself. Erin was sitting on the edge of the nest with Burt and Cal sitting beside her. Mama and Papa Seagull were sitting on the ledge, basking in the warm sunlight.

"Look at the waves down on the beach," said Erin.

Burt and Cal looked down and admired the view. The waves were breaking on the rocks below and sending large sheets of spray high into the air. The sunlight glinted off the spray droplets like shining jewels. The glittering jewels then slowly cascaded back down into the ocean. The sight was beautiful to behold.

"Dusty," said Burt, "come up here and look down at the beach. You've got to see this. It's really neat."

Dusty had no idea what the beach looked like. He had never climbed up onto the edge of the nest and looked down at the beach. He had really only looked at the ledge that the nest sat upon, and the bluffs which towered overhead. The thought had never occurred to him to climb onto the edge and look down.

"Don't sit next to me," said Erin, "I'm comfortable, and I don't want to move."

Dusty clambered up onto the edge of the nest and sat down next to Cal. He looked down and suddenly became very dizzy and disorientated. It was as if the world was spinning around out of control, and it made his stomach upset and queasy. He thought he was going to throw up. Dusty lost his balance and fell backwards into the nest. Erin laughed at him.

"Dusty!" cried Mama Seagull in alarm as she watched him topple into the nest. She jumped up onto the edge of the nest, and then hopped down inside to see what was wrong. She covered Dusty's shaking body with her wing to comfort him. Papa Seagull jumped up onto the edge of the nest and looked down inside at Mama and Dusty.

"What happened, dear?" asked Mama Seagull.

"I went to look down at the beach, Mama, when everything started spinning. My tummy doesn't feel good," responded Dusty.

"You were okay until you looked down, is that right?" asked Mama Seagull.

"Yeah, I was okay until I looked down. I feel strange."

"It's okay dear, close your eyes and you'll feel better."

Mama Seagull turned her head and looked up at Papa Seagull with

THE SEAGULL WHO WAS AFRAID TO FLY

concern in her eyes. *This is not good.*

"Is he gonna die, Papa?" asked Cal.

"No son, he's not going to die. Dusty is going to be all right."

"What's the matter with him, Mama?" asked Burt.

"I don't know, dear," said Mama. "I've never seen this happen before."

Everyone looked at Papa Seagull for an answer. He thought he knew what was wrong with Dusty, but he hoped that he was wrong. That thought sent a shiver through his body. It was something that simply did not happen to birds.

"I think that Dusty is afraid of heights," said Papa Seagull.

Chapter Two

There was a moment of stunned silence as everyone looked at each other in shock. Then they all looked down at Dusty. No one was really quite sure what the implications of Dusty's fear meant. They only knew that it couldn't be good.

"If Dusty is scared of heights, does that also mean that he'll be scared to fly?" asked Burt.

"I don't know," responded Papa Seagull. "I hope he's not afraid of flying."

"Is Dusty going to get well again?" asked Cal.

"He'll be fine dear," said Mama Seagull. "As long as he doesn't look down, he won't get sick." *I hope.*

"He'll never fly!" announced Erin. "He'll always be too scared. A seagull that can't fly will never be good for anything. Everybody knows that."

"Be quiet Erin!" said Mama Seagull angrily. She gave Erin a hard, cold, keep-your-mouth-shut look. It worked.

Erin indignantly turned around and sat down facing the sea. Her tail feathers were pointed straight at Dusty. *She* knew that she was superior to Dusty in every way. *She* was older. *She* was smarter. *She* knew the difference between a pelican and a dragon. *She* was not afraid of heights. She started the process of preening her feathers. She felt very smug.

As daylight faded and the sun slowly set beneath the horizon, the young seagulls slowly fell asleep, all except for Dusty. He no longer felt sick, but he lay down next to Cal, with his eyes open, looking up at the evening sky. The stars twinkled as they looked down on him from the nighttime sky. Dusty usually enjoyed looking at the stars, but tonight the stars gave him no comfort.

Mama and Papa Seagull sat on the ledge next to the nest. They were very concerned about Dusty. This was a circumstance that they were unprepared for.

"What will we do if he refuses to fly?" asked Mama

"He has to fly, if he's going to survive," said Papa. "It's the way of seagulls."

"But dear, how do we get Dusty to fly, when he can't even look down?"

"I don't know. I've never heard of this problem in a seagull before. It's something that Dusty will have to work out for himself. If he doesn't, he'll never survive. He will die."

"That's what I'm afraid of, dear. He has to be able to take care of himself, without the ability to fly. No one has ever done that, and lived. I want Dusty to grow up to be a normal seagull."

"So do I, so do I. But we can't *make* Dusty fly. He has to *want* to fly. What about Erin, Burt, and Cal—are they ready to fly?"

"Yes dear. The three of them could fly anytime. Their wings are all strong enough now."

"Perhaps it's time to kick them all out of the nest. Perhaps that will convince Dusty to fly."

"I know that it's probably time for them to leave. But I hate to see my babies go," said Mama as she softly started to cry.

"Tomorrow then," said Papa as he put his wing around Mama, "everyone will leave the nest. We'll dismantle it so that Dusty has no reason to stay. Let's hope he decides to fly away with us."

Dusty sat in the dark nest listening to his parents. He didn't know what to do. Their words disturbed him. Tomorrow he would be on his own. He knew he couldn't fly. If he flew, he would have to look down. Since he couldn't look down, he couldn't fly. He felt worthless and inferior.

What little sleep he got was fitful. He dreamt that he was falling, and woke up in a cold sweat. Visions of waves crashing upon the rocks filled his thoughts. It took a while for him to fall asleep again.

The dawn was bright and clear and there was a soft, warm breeze gently blowing the morning air. It was a glorious day, for everyone except Dusty.

"Rise and shine everybody," said Mama Seagull. "Come on you sleepy heads, wake up, wake up."

All of the young seagulls yawned and stretched and slowly rubbed the sleep out of their eyes. Dusty was worried, because he knew what was going to happen today. He had also gotten very little sleep. Papa Seagull waited and watched until everyone was wide awake.

Papa Seagull cleared his throat in preparation for his speech. As soon as he saw that he had everyone's attention, he began. "Today you are going to learn how to fly. Today you are going to leave the nest forever. Today you will truly become seagulls."

Papa Seagull swelled with pride. He had practiced that speech for weeks, in preparation for this moment. He thought he had said it rather well. He had put the right voice inflections on the right words. He had emphasized the word, *today*, each time he said it. All of a sudden, he thought about Dusty. What had Dusty been thinking as he heard the speech? With a silent groan, he looked at Dusty.

Everyone else also turned and looked at Dusty. Dusty wished that he could become invisible. His wish did not come true.

"What's going to happen to Dusty?" asked Burt.

"That depends on Dusty," said Papa Seagull. "We hope that he will try to fly today, but don't worry about him, he'll be all right."

Mama Seagull gave Erin a warning look. Erin was about to say something, but she saw the look on Mama's face and changed her mind. That turned out to be a wise decision. Erin loved to scold others, but she didn't like to get scolded herself. Dusty was relieved that he had been spared Erin's comments.

"Ok everybody, out of the nest," said Papa Seagull. "You too, Dusty."

Everybody climbed out of the nest and stood on the ledge. Papa Seagull walked over to where Erin was standing, and with no warning, pushed her off the ledge. Erin was too startled to be mad, and instinctively spread her wings. Her wings caught the updraft of air rising up the bluffs and she soared into the morning sky.

Erin was ecstatic. The exhilaration of flight was pure bliss. She flapped her wings and was amazed at how easy it was to fly. She flew away down the beach without a second thought about her family. She was actually pleased to be away from them.

"Wow!" exclaimed Burt. "Can we do that too, Papa?"

"Yes you can Burt. Just spread your wings and jump off the ledge. The air current will do the rest."

Burt walked to the edge of the ledge and spread his wings. He didn't get a chance to jump because the air currents caught his wings and lifted him straight up into the air. Burt was so surprised to find himself being lifted up into the sky that he started to flap his wings. Suddenly he was flying, and he loved it.

Cal imitated Burt's actions and soon he was flying off, trying to catch up with Burt. Dusty watched them fly off with a heavy heart. He wished that he could fly, but he knew that he couldn't. His heart was heavy with disappointment.

"Dusty," said Papa Seagull with a gentle voice, "we're not going to force you to fly. It would be too traumatic an experience for you right now. But you can't stay here. You must learn to survive on your own. This ledge gradually slopes down to the beach. Follow the ledge down, and you'll come to the beach. You must go now."

Dusty scrutinized the ledge for a moment, and then he looked back at his parents. Mama Seagull had tears in her eyes, and Papa Seagull looked worried.

"Goodbye Mama, Goodbye Papa," said Dusty in a trembling voice.

"Take care of yourself Dusty," said Mama Seagull. "And always remember that I love you."

"Good luck Dusty," said Papa Seagull. "Someday, you will conquer your fears, and you will fly."

Dusty turned around and started walking down the ledge. He had a long way to go, before he would reach the beach. Mama and Papa Seagull watched him go. Papa put his wing around Mama and tried to give her some comfort. Mama Seagull cried for a little while.

"It's time to dismantle the nest," said Papa Seagull. "We don't want

Dusty to have a reason to return here and stay. He would never survive here on his own."

Pulling the nest apart was tedious work. It had been well constructed. They pulled bits and pieces and fragments from the nest, and tossed them over the side. Some of the larger pieces required both of their efforts to push them over the ledge. The dried mud had made the nest rather heavy.

By noon, the last remaining segment went over the edge. With a heavy sigh, they opened their wings and flew away. As they flew off, Mama Seagull kept looking back to see if she could locate Dusty. She did not see him. The ledge quickly disappeared from sight as they flew off along the beach.

Dusty saw them fly away off in the distance, and a lump formed in his throat. He stopped walking and sat down. The tears that formed in his eyes fell freely. He cried until he could cry no more. He closed his eyes and tried not to think.

After a while, Dusty rose to his feet and continued slowly walking along the ledge. His steps were slow and his heart was heavy. As the sun was beginning to set, he came across a plant growing out of a crack in the ledge. He decided that this would be a good place to stop for the night. He squeezed in between the plant and the rock wall of the bluff. The plant sheltered him from the night wind, and gave him a small feeling of safety.

Dusty found some stalks of grass growing behind the plant and he promptly ate them. They tasted terrible, but his stomach wasn't quite so empty now. He sat down and tucked his head underneath his wing. Listening to the sounds of the night, Dusty slowly fell asleep.

The sky was bright, and the air was crisp and clean, with a scent of salt rising from the beach. Dusty awoke feeling both hungry and thirsty. He yawned and let the sleepiness slowly recede from his body. He licked the dew off the leaves of the plant until he was no longer thirsty. He then ate some more of the grass, which abated his appetite.

Dusty stood up and walked out from behind the plant and stood on the ledge. With a mighty yawn, he stretched out his wings and his legs. Today was a new day; perhaps he would reach the beach before sunset.

He certainly hoped so, as he resumed his trek along the ledge. He wondered about what he would do, once he reached the beach.

The ledge was slowly becoming wider as Dusty walked along. It took him a while to notice that fact, but he was surprised when he did. The ledge was now about three feet wide. He looked at the ledge ahead of him, but it did not seem to get any wider. Dusty shrugged his shoulders and continued walking.

After walking for about another hour, he came upon a pile of rocks that were blocking the ledge. He looked up and could see where the rocks had fallen from the bluffs. At first he tried to climb over the rocks, but that didn't work. The rocks simply came tumbling down around him. His webbed feet just weren't made for climbing. He stood back and surveyed the rocks. Then an idea popped into his head.

He pushed against one of the rocks that had tumbled down, and found that he could roll it right over the edge of the ledge. One by one, he started pushing rocks over the edge. In a few hours, he had cleared a path along the edge of the ledge. He pushed one more rock over the edge, and found himself on the other side of the rockslide. He walked back away from the edge and sat down to rest.

Dusty was exhausted from his exertions. He had been careful not to look down while he was working along the edge of the ledge. He had actually been too busy pushing rocks to look down. When he thought about it, he realized that he had indeed watched some of the rocks go over the ledge. But he also knew that he had not watched them as they fell downward. It was however, a small victory for Dusty. He felt much better about himself as he rested in the shade of the rocks.

When he felt sufficiently rested, he started walking along the ledge again. He was both hungry and thirsty, but there was nothing he could do about that. He had been walking for a couple of hours when he came across his next obstacle. A tree branch lay across the ledge.

The tree branch was lying diagonally across the ledge, pointing away from Dusty. About one-third of the branch, including the limb, stuck out over the ledge, and the remaining two-thirds lay on the ledge. The branch completely blocked Dusty's advancement down the ledge.

Dusty looked straight up and saw a tree high above him at the top of the bluff. That explained where the branch had come from. Dusty shook his head in disbelief. He couldn't believe how bad his luck was. First he had to leave the nest. Second was the pile of rocks. Now there was a tree branch blocking his path. He sat down and stared at the tree branch.

As Dusty was scrutinizing the branch, he noticed for the first time that there were bugs crawling all over it. His stomach growled. He realized just how hungry he actually was. Dusty feasted on the various insects crawling around on the branch. When his tummy was full, he sat down, made himself comfortable, and fell asleep. He slept soundly until the next morning.

The sunlight filtering through the branches woke Dusty in the morning. He was surprised to have slept so much. He didn't realize just how tired he had been. He licked the dew off the dead leaves on the branch, and quenched his thirst. He ate some more of the bugs until his tummy was full again. He then stepped back and studied the tree branch. There was no way to get around the branch. He would have to go though the middle.

Dusty started pushing his way between the branch and the wall of the bluff. He was making his way through, when he felt the branch start to quiver. He gingerly pushed against some twigs and felt the whole branch jerk backward in response. The branch trembled for a moment, and then slowly started to move.

The branch was slowly starting to swing backwards out over the ledge. In an instant of sheer terror, Dusty realized that the branch was swinging in his direction. It would sweep him right over the ledge. He turned around and ran as fast as he could. He could hear the branch scraping against the bluff as it picked up speed. The noise of scraping twigs and leaves became louder. He knew that he wasn't running fast enough. The branch was catching up with him. Seagull legs aren't made for running, and suddenly Dusty tripped and fell down. The only thing he could think to do was to cover his eyes with his wings.

Dusty heard the roar of the branch as it swept across the rock just inches above his body. He felt the whoosh of air against his feathers. If his feet hadn't gotten tangled up with each other, causing him to fall down, Dusty would have been killed. Falling down had saved his life. The branch swept over his inert body and fell over the ledge, loudly crashing down onto the beach below. Dusty lay on the ledge, shaking, as he realized just how close to death he had come. He slowly stood to his feet, and leaned back against the rock wall.

Dusty breathed deeply for a few minutes, and slowly regained his composure. He was tempted to look over the edge, down at the fallen branch. He quickly decided against that, and instead, started walking along the ledge again. If this was excitement and adventure, he could do without it.

The ledge began sloping downward at a steeper angle. Dusty found that he had to carefully watch his step to prevent himself from falling. He soon lost track of time. As a result, he was concentrating so hard on his footing, that it took him a while to realize that the ledge had ended. He was on the beach at last.

Dusty was so happy that he started to dance. Never mind that he did not know how to dance, or that dancing is very difficult when you have webbed feet. He was ecstatic. He kicked his legs out and swung his wings around. He was in the process of executing a pirouette, when he noticed the two old crabs intently watching him.

Chapter Three

Dusty's momentum carried him through another complete spin before he came to a stop. He slowly spun to a stop facing the crabs, with his right foot sticking straight out, his right wing pointing straight up, and his left wing pointing down. It was actually a splendid movement that would have brought a normal audience to its feet in a standing ovation. The two old crabs did not seem to be impressed. Apparently the two crabs were not a normal audience.

Dusty just stood there gawking at the two old crabs. Then he realized that his body was still gesturing in a rather ridiculous position. He put his right foot back down on the ground, and pulled his wings back up against his body. He realized that his mouth was open, so he closed it. He felt extremely foolish.

The two old crabs turned and looked at each other. Their expressionless faces revealed nothing about what they were thinking. Without a word, they then turned back and gazed at Dusty again. One of the crabs had a golden yellow shell, while the other crab had a dark orange shell. The color of their shells was the only difference that Dusty could see between the two crabs. Since Dusty had never been around crabs before, they all looked pretty much the same to him.

The yellow crab turned to the orange crab and said in a rasping voice, "Well, there's something you don't see every day, a dancing seagull."

"Now I've seen everything," responded the orange crab in a tired, almost wheezing voice. "I can now die in peace."

"You'll die in pieces, at the rate you're going," responded the yellow crab.

THE SEAGULL WHO WAS AFRAID TO FLY

"If I had any energy, I'd teach you some manners, you old windbag," said the orange crab.

"Windbag! Windbag! Call me a windbag will you?"

Dusty saw that the two old crabs had forgotten all about him, and he decided to leave. He took a couple of steps backward to see if the crabs were paying any attention to him. His movement caught their attention. If he would have remained perfectly still, it is quite possible that the two crabs would have forgotten all about him, and left.

The crabs stopped shouting at each other (if you could call it shouting) and walked up close to Dusty and resumed staring at him. Dusty felt very uncomfortable having the two old crabs staring at him like that. He nervously cleared his throat. He decided to introduce himself.

"Hello, my name is Dusty," he said very timidly.

"I'm Flim," said the yellowed-shelled crab after a moment of silence.

"I'm Flam," said the orange-shelled crab.

"We're brothers," they both said simultaneously.

"We usually live alone and keep to ourselves," said Flim.

"We're Hermit Crabs," said Flam.

"What's a Hermit Crab?" asked Dusty.

The two old crabs looked at each in disbelief. They looked back at Dusty for a moment. They looked back at each other. They sighed.

"A hermit is a crab who has withdrawn himself from crab society," said Flim.

"We prefer a solitary existence," said Flam.

"I wouldn't stick around here if I were you," said Flim.

"Why not?" asked Dusty.

"Because, the sky is falling!" said Flam.

Dusty looked up at the sky and observed it for a moment. It seemed to be staying in place. He had no idea what would happen if the sky actually fell down, but he thought that it would probably be extremely disastrous. He wondered if the world would come to an end if that happened. Then he began to wonder about the sanity of the crabs.

"It doesn't look like the sky is falling," said Dusty.

"Oh it doesn't, does it?" responded Flim.
"I don't think he believes us," said Flam.
"Looks can be deceiving, boy," said Flim.
"Don't always trust your eyes," said Flam
"Sit down young boy," said Flim.
"And we'll tell you a tale of woe," said Flam.
"A tale of destruction," added Flim.
"A tale of horror!" exclaimed Flam.
Flim turned to Flam and exclaimed, "Must you be so theatrical?"
"I wasn't being theatrical, I was being . . . dramatic," said Flam.
"Don't overdo it," said Flim.
"Humph," said Flam.
"Anyway boy, it's a tale that will convince you," said Flim while waving his claws in the air, "that the sky is indeed, falling."
"Talk about theatrics," muttered Flam.

Flim gave Flam a dirty look, which silenced him. Dusty sat down and made himself comfortable. He wasn't at all sure about these two old crabs. They were very eccentric and kind of peculiar. The crabs waited until they saw that Dusty was seated and paying attention to them. They then proceeded to tell their story.

"Three days ago we were at the base of the bluff," said Flim.
"Eating breakfast, in the morning," said Flam.
"When all of a sudden," said Flim.
"Wham!" said Flam as he crashed his claw noisily onto the ground for effect.
"What did I tell you about theatrics?" asked Flim
"Look who's talking," responded Flam.
"You can imagine our surprise," continued Flim.
"At having our breakfast so rudely interrupted," said Flam.
"Anyway, pieces of a nest started falling from the sky," said Flim.
"Right on top of us," said Flam.
"Some of the chunks were rather large," said Flim.
"The size of boulders," said Flam.
"The sound was like thunder," said Flim.
"We barely escaped with our lives!" said Flam.

THE SEAGULL WHO WAS AFRAID TO FLY

Dusty sat there thinking to himself. It was three days ago that he had left the nest. Mama and Papa had probably taken the nest apart and pushed the pieces over the ledge. Flim and Flam must have been directly underneath the nest. It was almost too much of a coincidence. Dusty looked up and noticed that the two old crabs were intently watching him.

"I'm sorry," apologized Dusty. "Please continue with your story."

"Yes, well, the rest of the day we moved along the bluff," said Flim.

"To get away from falling nests," said Flam.

"Nothing else fell on us the rest of the day," said Flim

"We thought we were safe," said Flam.

"The next morning, we were eating our breakfast," said Flim.

"Minding our own business," said Flam.

"And do you know what happened?" asked Flim.

Dusty thought he knew the answer but wisely shook his head, just in case he was wrong.

"You probably wouldn't be able to guess anyway," said Flam.

"So you can imagine our surprise," said Flim.

"At having breakfast rudely interrupted again," said Flam.

"By rocks falling out of the sky," answered Flim.

"They were the size of boulders!" exclaimed Flam.

"The sound was like thunder," said Flim.

"Without the lightning," said Flam.

"The rocks were bouncing around everywhere," said Flim.

"We barely escaped with our lives!" said Flam.

"As you can imagine, it's very difficult to eat your breakfast when rocks start raining down on your head," said Flim.

"It's also very difficult to stay alive," said Flam.

"We're not as young and fast as we used to be," said Flim.

Dusty knew that there was no coincidence now. He had spent time pushing rocks from the rockslide off the ledge two mornings ago. He remembered how tiring that work had been. He had no idea that the two crabs had been directly below him. He felt slightly guilty.

"So we moved along the base of the bluff to get away from the falling rocks," said Flam.

27

"We thought we found a good safe place to spend the night," said Flim.

"So we did," said Flam.

"We were eating our breakfast this morning," said Flim.

"Minding our own business," said Flam.

"When we heard a noise directly above us," said Flim.

"It was the noise of horror," said Flam.

"Imagine our surprise when we looked up," said Flim.

"And saw a tree falling down on top of us," said Flam, menacingly.

"The sound was like thunder,"said Flim.

"We ran as fast as we could," said Flam.

"It's not good to run with your mouth full," said Flim.

"We barely escaped alive," said Flam.

"So we walked along the base of the bluff all day until we found you," said Flim.

"It's no longer safe for a crab to eat breakfast anymore," said Flam.

Dusty knew that the "tree" which had fallen this morning was actually the branch that he had pushed off the ledge. He knew that he had been responsible for the "sky" falling. He wasn't sure whether or not he should say anything about this to Flim and Flam. He decided that he would wait until the two old crabs were in a better mood. It might be best if they did not know that *he* was the source of their problems. Once again the crabs had stopped talking while Dusty was thinking to himself, and they stood there, regarding him.

"We'll show you where we're spending the night," said Flim.

"If you'd like to see it, that is," said Flam.

"Um, yes, I'd like that," responded Dusty.

The two crabs led Dusty to a small opening in the base of the cliff wall. It was actually a small cave, but it had plenty of room inside for Dusty to walk without having to duck his head. The crabs were obviously very pleased with their cave.

"We found this cave today," said Flim.

"A few hours before you walked down the ledge," said Flam.

"It's very nice," said Dusty.

"Thank you," said Flim. "Would you like to stay for dinner?"

"If you're hungry," said Flam.

"Yes I am hungry, and yes I would like to stay for dinner," responded Dusty.

"We may be Hermit Crabs," said Flim.

"But we can still be polite," said Flam.

"When we want to be," said Flim.

"We're having fish for dinner," said Flam.

"Do you like fish?" asked Flim.

"Oh yes, I like fish very much," responded Dusty.

"Do you like it cooked or uncooked?" asked Flam.

"You cook fish?" asked Dusty.

"No," said Flim, "but it would be impolite not to ask."

"Oh, I see," said Dusty, who clearly did not.

The crabs brought out some fish that they had stashed in the cave before they found Dusty. It was a genuine feast for Dusty. Everyone ate until they were full. When they were finished eating, the two old crabs sat back and gazed at Dusty again.

"So tell us, Dusty, what were you doing on that ledge anyway?" asked Flim.

Dusty told them the story about being afraid of heights. He told them about Mama and Papa teaching the others how to fly, while he could not. He told them about his journey down the ledge. But he conveniently left out the details about the nest, rocks, and branch. There was no sense in getting the two old crabs all excited again. When he was done, the crabs sat there with thoughtful expressions on their faces.

"Where will you go?" asked Flim.

"What will you do?" asked Flam.

"I don't know," answered Dusty thoughtfully. "I have to find a way to get over my fear of heights. I have to learn how to fly. I need someone to help me."

"Well, we can't help you," said Flim.

"We're only crabs," said Flam.

"You need someone who can fly to help you," said Flim.

"Crabs don't fly very well," said Flam.

"We can offer you a place to spend the night, however," said Flim.

"You can spend the night with us," said Flam.

"You can resume your journey after breakfast," said Flim.

"If the sky doesn't fall on us, that is," said Flam.

"Thank you," said Dusty. "You're both very kind."

"I'd appreciate it if you kept that opinion to yourself," said Flim.

"We don't want you to ruin our reputation, you understand," said Flam.

"Your secret is safe with me," laughed Dusty.

"And if you ever tell anybody that we're not crotchety old crabs," said Flim.

"We'll tell everybody what a lousy dancer you are," said Flam.

The three of them broke out laughing. It turned out to be the best night's sleep that Dusty had gotten in several days. Dusty woke up refreshed and ready to be on his way. Life was turning out to be a rather big adventure. There was no telling what each day had in store. As he ate breakfast, he noticed that the two old crabs kept nervously looking out the cave's opening.

"Well, I must be going now," announced Dusty. "I think that the two of you will be quite safe here in the cave, at least until after breakfast. The sky doesn't seem to fall after breakfast. Thank you both very much for taking care of me. I won't forget your kindness."

"You're welcome, Dusty," said Flim. "Come back anytime."

"Be careful when you step outside," said Flam.

"You never know what may fall on your head," said Flim.

Dusty walked outside the cave and made a big show of looking up at the sky. It was the least he could do for the two old crabs. He liked them very much.

"It's safe outside," Dusty shouted into the cave. "There's nothing falling from the sky, today."

"He's a good lad," said Flim's voice.

"Even if he can't dance," responded Flam's voice.

Dusty laughed and started walking toward the ocean. He jokingly walked along with his head pointing up, looking for falling objects. He wasn't watching where he was walking or where he was going. The

THE SEAGULL WHO WAS AFRAID TO FLY

beach was covered with small rocks, and driftwood had washed up all around. It is usually a good idea to watch where you're walking, especially on a rock-strewn beach. This was however, a lesson that Dusty had not yet learned.

Suddenly Dusty bumped into another seagull, causing them both to fall down. The other seagull had also been looking up, trying to see what it was that Dusty was looking at. Dusty picked himself up and found himself face to face with the prettiest young seagull he had ever seen.

Chapter Four

Once again, Dusty found himself in an embarrassing situation. It is one thing to bump into a pretty lady, but it's quite another when you both fall down. It's definitely not the recommended way to meet new people. It does, however, give new meaning to the phrase "you'll never guess who I just bumped into." Dusty clumsily clambered back up onto his feet, and then helped the pretty seagull onto hers. He was very embarrassed.

Dusty found himself spellbound by her beauty. She still had her gray feathers, which meant that she was Dusty's age or perhaps just a little older. Her eyes sparkled in the sunlight and she had long, beautiful eyelashes. Dusty found himself captivated by her winning smile.

"I'm, I'm, really sorry about that," stammered Dusty. "I didn't mean to knock you down."

"It's really my fault," responded the pretty seagull in a soft velvety voice. "I was looking up to see what you were looking at and, well, here we are. What were you looking at, anyway?"

"Well, I was looking up to see if the sky was falling. What I mean is, I was checking to see if anything was falling from the sky. Not that I was expecting anything to fall! I'm not making any sense am I?" *I can't believe I just said that!*

"No," laughed the pretty seagull.

"It's a long story," said Dusty. He was desperate; there had to be some way he could save his image. If first impressions are important, he was in trouble. He realized that he had to do something to save this situation.

"Perhaps we should just start over again. "Hi, my name is Dusty. It's a pleasure to meet you," said Dusty as he gave her a bow and a flourish with his wing.

"My name is Jill, and it certainly is pleasure to meet you, Dusty. You are the first interesting seagull I've met since I left the nest. And I would love to hear your story."

Dusty looked at Jill, and decided to trust her. So he told her his story, starting with the nest, and ended with leaving Flim and Flam's cave and bumping (literally) into her. He left nothing out, and even told her about his fear of heights. Jill listened to Dusty's story with rapt attention. When Dusty finished, Jill continued to gaze at him in silence. Suddenly, she broke out laughing.

"You are the first person I have ever met, who could make the sky fall," laughed Jill. "I can just see those two old crabs running around trying to dodge falling rocks. And can you imagine the expression on their faces when they looked up and saw a tree falling straight at them? I'll bet their eyes just about popped out their sockets, they were so big."

Jill doubled over with laughter. She started laughing so hard that tears flowed from her eyes. Her laughter was contagious, and soon Dusty was laughing right along with her. As he imagined Flim and Flam dodging objects that he had unwittingly tossed on top them, he began to see the absurdity of it all. When they finally stopped laughing, they had to sit back and recover their breath.

"I thought that you might laugh at me for being afraid to fly," said Dusty shyly.

"No Dusty," responded Jill. "Everyone is afraid of something. Just because you are afraid to fly, does not mean that you are not special. I believe that someday you will learn how to fly."

They stopped talking and watched another young seagull fly past them. That seagull looked somewhat familiar to Dusty. He had a bad feeling about this but he couldn't quite figure out why. The seagull circled around Dusty and Jill several times and then landed beside them. The newcomer tucked its wings and strutted up to them. It was Erin. Dusty groaned. Not her, not now! Erin's presence made him feel nervous.

"Well, well, well, I'm surprised to see that you're still alive," said

Erin.

"I'm glad to see you too, sister," said Dusty in a sarcastic voice.

Erin regarded him with a disdainful expression. "I saw a seagull with a broken wing," said Erin. "He died because he couldn't fly and find food. You'll die, too." Her eyes narrowed with contempt. "You're too stupid and scared to fly."

"This rude thing is your sister?" asked Jill.

"Unfortunately," responded Dusty.

Erin walked in a circle around Jill, scrutinizing her very closely and critically. Jill was quickly becoming very indignant with Erin, and wondered how Dusty had put up with such a rude sister. Dusty wanted to find a hole to crawl into and hide. He did not want to be around Erin, especially since she was being such a snob today. Then he realized that Erin had always been arrogant. She had always been a snob.

"And just who do we have here?" said Erin to Jill.

"None of your business," responded Jill.

Without knowing that he was doing it, Dusty moved closer to Jill until they were standing side by side. Jill and Erin both noticed what Dusty was doing. Jill was touched, and impressed by Dusty's action. Erin however, was outraged. Dusty and Jill were facing Erin, but their backs were to the sea.

"Oh, so you think you're going to protect your girlfriend from me, do you Dusty?" said Erin venomously.

"Go away Erin," said Dusty. "You're an arrogant snob and you're not in charge here."

"Oh really," responded Erin. "You're just a seagull who's too afraid to even fly. Well I'm not afraid of you."

"You should be," said a hoarse voice from behind Erin.

Erin spun around and found herself face to face with the two old crabs. They were menacingly moving toward her with their claws wide open. The two old crabs looked mean and ferocious. Erin looked at their claws and knew that she was in trouble. She was used to bossing people around and being a bully. Now that the tables were turned, she didn't know what to do.

"Always be afraid of picking on someone," said Flim.

THE SEAGULL WHO WAS AFRAID TO FLY

"Who has friends who will stick up for him," said Flam.

"She looks young and tender," said Flim as he gave Dusty a wink.

"Tender, juicy meat I'll bet," agreed Flam.

"I think she'll taste quite good," said Flim.

"We'll feast tonight," said Flam.

At that comment, Erin took off shrieking in terror. She flew away as fast as her wings could carry her. Flim and Flam burst out laughing as she flew away, and slapped each other on the shells with their claws in glee.

"Thank you for helping out," said Dusty. "Your timing was perfect."

"Glad to be of assistance," said Flim.

"We watch out for our friends," said Flam.

"I'd like you to meet Jill," said Dusty. "She's also my friend. We just met this morning."

Flim and Flam exchanged knowing looks.

"You must be Flim and Flam," said Jill. "Dusty has told me all about you. He's lucky to have two good friends. It certainly is a pleasure to meet you. Can I ask you a question?"

"Go right ahead, young lady," said Flim.

"Ask away," said Flam.

"Would you really have eaten her?" asked Jill.

"No, we couldn't have," said Flim.

"We're too slow to catch her," said Flam.

"And besides, we don't like the taste of seagull," said Flim.

"Tastes like chicken," said Flam.

"Yuck!" they both said simultaneously, with foul expressions on their faces. Then they both broke out in laughter. They laughed until they had tears in their eyes. They had to sit down to catch their breath. After a bit of chuckling, the two crabs got back up onto their feet.

"Well, you two lovebirds take it easy," said Flim.

"We're off to get some real food," said Flam.

"It was good to meet you, Jill," said Flim.

"Take good care of Dusty for us," said Flam.

Without a further word, both crabs walked into the waves and soon disappeared underneath the surface of the water. Dusty and Jill stood still and watched them go. Dusty doubted that he would ever see Erin again. He wasn't sure that he ever wanted to see her again. He was thankful for the intervention of Flim and Flam. A thought occurred to him. He turned to look at Jill.

"What's a lovebird?" asked Dusty.

"Don't you worry about it," she said as she smiled sweetly at him. "Come on, I want you to meet a friend of mine."

Jill started to wade out into the ocean. She turned around and motioned for Dusty to follow her. "Come on Dusty, let's go for a swim."

"I don't know how to swim."

"It's easy, and I'll teach you. Come out to where I'm standing."

Dusty started wading out into the water to where Jill was standing, waiting for him. The cool water felt strange on his legs and feet. It was a totally new sensation. Jill reached out her wing to him.

"Hold my wing, Dusty. We're going to do this together. When the next wave comes in, it will lift us up. When you feel yourself floating, start paddling your feet; it will propel you forward. You'll be surprised at what these webbed feet can do."

The next wave came in and lifted them up. Dusty started paddling with his feet and quickly started swimming out to sea. He held onto Jill's wing for a few minutes until he felt comfortable swimming. It was incredibly easy. By turning his feet, he could change the direction that he was moving. And it was fun!

"Where are we going?" asked Dusty.

"Do you see that large buoy out there? That's where we're headed."

"Your friend is out there?"

"That's where he is alright, you'll see him when we get there. Don't worry Dusty, you'll like him, and he'll like you."

It took them a couple of hours to slowly swim out to the buoy. The sight of it fascinated Dusty. As they swam up close, he could see a big sea lion lazily basking in the sun. The sea lion watched them as they swam up to the buoy.

"Hola Paco," said Jill.

THE SEAGULL WHO WAS AFRAID TO FLY

"Jill," said Paco with a heavy Mexican accent. "It is good to see you again. Who is your amigo?"

"This is Dusty. Do you mind if we join you?"

"No, no, not at all, you are welcome here anytime, come on up."

"Okay, Dusty, flap your wings hard, and push down with your feet against the water. Watch me, then do the same thing," said Jill.

Dusty watched Jill as she half jumped, half flew, up to where Paco was waiting. He took a deep breath. He flapped his wings as hard as he could, and shoved down hard with his feet. He flew up to where Jill and Paco were waiting and watching. Jill was ecstatic, and Dusty was surprised.

"You see Dusty, you can do it!"

"Wow! I sure did, but that was just a short hop. And I'm only a couple of feet above the water, so I'm really pretty low to the ground. I can easily look down from here without getting sick."

"I no comprende what the problema is here," said Paco.

"It's a long story," said Dusty. "But the problem is this: I'm afraid of heights so therefore, I'm afraid to fly."

"Ah," said Paco. "I too am afraid of flying. I don't think I would stay up in the air for very long. We sea lions don't float in the air so good. Too much blubber, I think. Can you imagine a sea lion trying to fly? It would be very ugly. I think I stay right here."

Everyone started to laugh. Dusty liked Paco and he could see why Jill liked to visit him. Dusty looked at Paco and admired his mustache. Paco's body was covered with a soft coat of short brown velvety fur. Dusty had never been around an animal as large as Paco, and he was quite impressed. But it wasn't just Paco's size that impressed Dusty, it was also his warm personality. It was pleasurable to listen to his thick Mexican accent. Paco's laid-back style made you want to relax and unwind. The world moved much slower on Paco's buoy.

"I still have some fish, though it's left over from lunch. Would you like some?" asked Paco.

"Yes we would," responded Dusty and Jill.

Paco smiled as he watched his two seagull friends eat their lunch. He seldom allowed seagulls on his buoy. Most seagulls were messy and noisy and worried about something or other. They were horrible gossips and enjoyed picking on each other. They seldom took the time to enjoy life. But Dusty and Jill were different. A seagull who was afraid to fly. Now that was something you didn't run across every day. He twirled his mustache with his flipper as he pondered Dusty's problem. His keen mind found a solution just as Dusty and Jill finished eating.

"I think I have the answer to your problema, Dusty."

Dusty sat down and paid close attention to Paco. Jill sat down next to Dusty and they waited for Paco to continue.

"Your problema seems to be that you do not like heights."

Dusty nodded his head.

"Why could you not simply fly low over the water and the ground? As long as you stay low, you not get sick."

Dusty pondered Paco's solution. It sounded simple. It made sense. It could work, if he could fly low. He turned and looked at Jill.

"Jill, is it possible for me to only fly low?"

"Sure it's possible, as long as you don't hit a strong gust of wind or a thermal updraft. If that happens, you can suddenly find yourself a lot higher up in the air than you, Dusty, would want to be. I know because it has happened to me," said Jill.

Dusty hung his head and groaned. The answer had been within his reach, but he could not grab it. Perhaps he would never fly. It seemed hopeless.

"I'm sorry, Dusty," said Jill. "If I knew that you could fly low without being accidentally lifted high up into the air, I would say that Paco's idea would work. But I can't make any guarantees. The last thing I want is for you to get hurt." Jill turned her head and looked at Paco. "Paco, can you come up with any more ideas?"

"I will give it some thought, my amigos," responded Paco.

Paco stretched his large body out on the warm buoy and stared out at the horizon. He absent-mindedly twirled his mustache with his flipper. It seemed to be a habit he had. Dusty and Jill made themselves comfortable as they waited. Since Paco never did anything in a hurry, they both knew that they would have to be patient.

THE SEAGULL WHO WAS AFRAID TO FLY

The afternoon sun warmed the buoy which caused it to give off a radiant heat. The heat made Dusty and Jill very drowsy. They patiently waited for Paco to think up a new idea. The two seagulls dozed off in the afternoon sun after a short period of time.

Paco looked at the sleeping birds and smiled. He shifted his gaze from the ocean to the shoreline. He looked at the bluffs off in the distance and studied the rock formations along the shore. He watched the lighthouse for awhile, but its lamp would not be illuminated until nightfall. His eyes kept returning to the lighthouse. An idea slowly started to form in the back of his mind. But then, Paco wasn't in a hurry, he never was. While looking at the lighthouse, Paco formulated a plan to cure Dusty's fear.

Paco rearranged his weight, and sat up. It took considerable effort. His movement caused the buoy to bounce around, waking Dusty and Jill from their slumber. Paco waited while they yawned and stretched. When they were fully awake, he outlined his plan.

"I have an idea about how to cure your fear of heights, Dusty," said Paco. "But it will require mucho work on your part. Do you see that lighthouse on top of the bluff?"

Dusty and Jill turned and looked at the lighthouse and nodded.

"Do you think you can get up there?" asked Paco.

"I think the ledge goes all the way up to the top. Yes, I should be able to get up there," answered Dusty. "But it will take us a few days to get there."

"Bueno," said Paco. "The hard part will be when you actually get up there, to the top. You must force yourself to look over the edge. Just a glance at first. Then, slowly increase the amount of time that you look down. When you get to the point where you can look down for a long time, you'll be ready to fly. I think you will be able to overcome your fear this way. Do you think you can do this, Dusty?"

"I don't know, Paco," responded Dusty. "I will give it a try. It's the least that I can do. If I don't try, I will never know."

"Not to worry, amigo," said Paco. "Jill will be with you and she will help you. It is sometimes a difficult journey to overcome fear, but I have mucho confidence in you."

"That's right, Dusty," said Jill. "We're in this together. We're friends, and that's what friends are for."

"Remember Dusty," said Paco, "just a little bit at a time. If you take it slowly, you will do it. Look at me, I no do anything in a hurry, and I take life slowly. So should you."

"Well I'm certainly in no hurry to look over the edge of a cliff," said Dusty. "But I will follow your advice, Paco. Would you mind if we came back to visit you, after I get over my fear of heights?"

"We are all amigos," said Paco. "You two are welcome here anytime. And I look forward to hearing about you conquering your fear."

"Thank you, Paco," said Jill. "You are a wonderful friend."

"Thank you, Paco," said Dusty. "It's been a pleasure to meet you, and I hope to fly here soon and thank you again."

"Adios amigos," said Paco. "Hasta la vista."

Dusty and Jill walked from the center of the buoy to the side that was facing the shore. Dusty nervously looked down at the water. He did not look forward to the long swim back to shore. Jill and Paco were quietly watching him. Jill had an idea.

"Dusty," said Jill. "I would like you to try something. I'd like you to try an extremely low level flight. At worst, you'll splash into the water, and then we'll have to swim back to shore. But if you can do it, and I think you can, we'll get to the shore in no time at all."

Dusty felt a lump in his throat, and butterflies in his stomach. He licked his beak and nodded his head. *I must be crazy!*

"Ok, let's do it, before I think about it and change my mind," said Dusty.

"Good luck Dusty," said Paco.

"Set your wings out like this," said Jill as she stretched out her wings as far as they would go. She watched Dusty spread out his wings. "Now jump off the buoy and let your body glide."

Dusty gathered up his courage and jumped off the buoy before he could change his mind, and found himself swiftly gliding across the waves. His courage quickly left as he skimmed above the waves. He felt the warm air as it rushed past his body. He found that he was terrified, but there was nothing he could do now except to continue to fly. There was no going back; he was committed now.

Jill jumped off the buoy and started flying after Dusty. She quickly caught up with him. She noticed that his eyes were closed.

"Open your eyes, Dusty, and look at me," said Jill.

Dusty opened his eyes which had been tightly shut and looked at Jill.

"Good, now look down at the waves and try to gauge how high you are above them."

"I think I'm about one foot above the waves," said Dusty as he looked down.

"Right, now flap your wings a couple of times, you're getting too low. We want to stay at about this height. How are you doing?"

"Okay I think, other than the fact that I'm terrified," responded Dusty as he flapped his wings.

They skimmed over the waves and Dusty was astonished at the speed they were doing. The sunlight sparkled off the waves and the light dazzled Dusty's eyes. The shore was approaching rather quickly and Dusty wanted to end his maiden flight as soon as possible. They crossed the shoreline and the rocky ground whizzed by underneath him. That was when Dusty realized that he didn't know how to stop. He didn't know how to land. The thought that perhaps he should stop flapping his wings never occurred. Dusty saw a large driftwood log looming directly in front of him. He had no idea how to stop or turn to avoid hitting the log. Dusty panicked as he rushed straight at the log. He knew that if he didn't do something very quickly, that this flight was going to end very painfully.

"Dusty pull up!" screamed Jill as she watched him zooming in toward the log. "Pull up now! Pull up!"

Chapter Five

Dusty crashed straight into the log. His momentum caused him to flip up and over the top of the log. He landed on his back on the other side. Jill flew to where he lay, and found him unconscious. She shook him and tried to wake him, without any success. She was just beginning to panic when a harp seal came running up to her.

"Wow, what a spectacular landing!" exclaimed the harp seal. His voice had a peculiar country twang that Jill had never heard before. "I thought that only gooney birds were capable of an impact like that. He really knocked himself out, didn't he?"

"He's unconscious and I don't know what to do," wailed Jill in desperation.

"Let's move him up against the log where we can keep him warm," said the harp seal. "As long as he's breathing, he should be okay."

The seal picked up Dusty and gently placed him next to the log. Jill sat down beside Dusty and used her body to keep him warm. She fretted and worried as she huddled next to Dusty's inert body. Jill did not look like she was in a mood to talk, so the seal remained silent. As the sun began to set, Jill found herself fighting to stay awake. The stress of Dusty's accident was taking its toll on her. The harp seal kept a watchful vigil while Jill dozed in a restless slumber.

Dusty awoke the next morning feeling the aches and pains caused by his abrupt landing. His head felt thick and fuzzy. He lay there wondering if he was dead. He shifted his weight, which caused him to let out a groan. His action woke up Jill.

"Dusty, are you all right?" asked Jill.

"I think so, but my body aches."

"I was worried about you. When you crashed into the log, I thought that you were seriously hurt. I'm so happy that you're okay."

Dusty stood up and stretched his wings and legs. His body was a little sore, especially his head, but nothing was broken. He was a little unsteady on his feet and he wobbled for a moment. He felt slightly better however, after he started walking around a little bit. Jill watched him closely, but she was obviously relieved.

"I don't think I'm cut out for flying," said Dusty.

"You fly just fine, it's your landing that we need to work on," said Jill.

"I hope you don't mind if we wait a few days before we try that again," said Dusty as he rubbed his head with his wing. "I don't know if I could survive the practice sessions."

"We'll wait until you get over your fear of heights," said Jill.

Just then the harp seal walked around the end of the log. He came up to Dusty and Jill and dropped a fish down on the ground. He took a good, long, appraising look at Dusty.

"Well, you're awake, alive, and up and about," said the seal. "Good, good, that's good to see. I brought you some breakfast. I thought you might be hungry."

"Thank you so very much," said Jill. "We never were properly introduced yesterday. My name is Jill, and this is Dusty."

"I'm Elvis," said the seal. "Eat up, and I'll tell you all about myself." He paused while Dusty and Jill started to eat. "I am a banjo playing harp seal."

"You play the banjo?" asked Dusty with his mouth full of food.

Jill nudged him with her wing, "Don't talk with your mouth full."

"That's right, I play the banjo," said Elvis. "You've never heard of me?"

Dusty and Jill both shook their heads. Elvis rubbed one of his long sideburns with his flipper and looked at Dusty and Jill with a confused expression on his face.

"You've never heard of me—Elvis?"

Once again Dusty and Jill shook their heads.

"Obviously my agent isn't doing his job," muttered Elvis. "I knew

I shouldn't have hired a turtle to handle my promotions campaign."

"Why do you need an agent?" asked Jill.

"Well you see, I'm a harp seal, and harp seals are the musically gifted branch of the seal family. I even have my own band. Right now we're headed down to Aqua World. We're going to get into show business. The way I see it, if a killer whale can make it big by doing flips and somersaults and other stupid Orca tricks, then me and my band will really hit it off big. I think that people would much rather be entertained by a singing harp seal playing a banjo, don't you? That's why I need an agent."

Dusty swallowed his last mouthful of food and asked, "You sing, too?"

"You bet I do. I'm very good, too, if I do say so myself. Are you sure you haven't heard of me? No? But lets not talk about me, I want to hear about you. So what's your story? Most birds don't fly head-on into logs like you did yesterday. Though I gotta admit, that was a spectacular entrance. I don't think that would work for me however, so I don't think I'll incorporate that entrance into my act. Did I hear Jill say that you were afraid of heights?"

"That's right," answered Dusty. "I am afraid of heights. I don't know why, but if I look down, from up high, I get sick. It first happened when I was still at home, in the nest. When I looked down, I got all dizzy and sick. I hadn't even tried to fly until yesterday. That was when I tried to fly for the first time. I tried a low level flight from Paco's buoy yesterday, but you saw how that turned out."

"Don't give up Dusty," said Elvis. "It took a lot of practice before I became proficient at playing the banjo. In much the same way, it will be the same with you. If you practice, you'll fly like an eagle. But I would recommend that you practice some place where there are no logs."

Dusty laughed along with Elvis.

"So you guys know Paco do you? I once wrote a song about him and his fellow sea lions. He never did like it, but then, sea lions don't really appreciate music, anyway. They don't have any rhythm. I think that comes from just lying around all day in the sun doing nothing. Would you two like to hear the song?"

"I'd love to hear you sing," said Jill. Dusty agreed along with her.

"Great," said Elvis as he started looking around. "Now where is my stage director?" Elvis put his flippers up to mouth and hollered, "Roy!"

A minute later, a sea otter came bounding up to Elvis. "What's up, boss?"

"Set up the stage and get the band ready," said Elvis to his stage director. "We're going to do a number. Tell the band that we're going to do the sea lion song."

"Right away, boss," replied Roy.

"Come on," said Elvis, "let's watch the crew set up the stage."

Roy bounded off, and Elvis, Dusty, and Jill walked around the log to watch the action. Jill was surprised to see so many animals because she had no idea that they had been there. She had thought that the only ones on the beach were herself, Dusty, and Elvis. Her eyes grew wide in wonder as she stood beside the log and watched. In a flurry of activity, a makeshift stage was erected and the band climbed up onto it and started setting up their instruments. The fiddler crabs tuned their violins and other harp seals tuned their saxophones, trumpets, and trombones. A couple of otters were tuning their guitars on another corner of the stage.

The noise was attracting a crowd. Seagulls, pelicans, geese, and ducks dropped in to enjoy the show. Seals, sea otters, walruses, and turtles swam ashore to get a good seat. Dusty looked around and was amazed at how big the crowd had become in such a short period of time. He had no idea that Elvis was so popular.

Roy, who was the stage director, walked up to the front of the stage. He gazed out over the audience for a moment and softly cleared his throat. He immediately had everyone's attention.

"Ladies and gentlemen," said Roy in a huge booming voice. "We'd like to welcome all sea mammals, aquatic birds, and crustaceans. And now," he paused for effect, "I present to you . . . the one . . . the only . . . banjo-playing harp seal . . . ELVIS!"

Dusty was shocked that anyone could speak so loudly. He watched Roy walk off the stage with awe and respect. He wondered if he could learn to speak with such a commanding voice.

"That's my cue," said Elvis as he headed for the stage.

Elvis walked to the center of the stage while the audience cheered and applauded. He picked up his banjo and walked up to the front of the stage and waited for the noise to die down. He bowed several times and seemed to enjoy the attention he was getting. His shiny black eyes quickly surveyed the audience. He loved being up on the stage in front of a crowd of fans. When the noise level dropped low enough, Elvis addressed his audience.

"Thank you very much," said Elvis in his quiet country accent. "Thank you, thank you and *thank you*," he said as he pointed to a female pelican. With a sigh, the female pelican fell over and fainted. Dusty raised his eyebrows in surprise as he watched the pelican faint.

"We're gonna do a song that we've never performed in public before," continued Elvis. "You folks are the first audience that we have ever played this song to. Are you ready for a treat?" He waited once again for the cheering and applause to die down. "I'd like to dedicate this song to Dusty and Jill, my two seagull friends who are right up here in the front row."

Dusty heard a young voice behind him say, "Wow, mom, they know Elvis!" Dusty was tempted to turn around and look, but decided that it would be impolite. He grinned at Jill, at then focused on Elvis.

Elvis turned to face the band and started snapping his flipper. "One, two, a one two three four."

The drummer continued the rock-and-roll beat, and the brass section started playing. The violins jumped in with a counter melody and the audience members started tapping their feet in time to the music. The music blended rock-and-roll and jazz into a unique and delightful medley. The whole beach resounded with music. Elvis waited for the intro to finish, and then he started to sing.

> *You ain't nothing but a sea lion, lying on a buoy.*
> *You ain't nothing but a sea lion, lying on a buoy.*
> *Well you ain't never caught a salmon and you ain't no friend of mine.*

THE SEAGULL WHO WAS AFRAID TO FLY

Elvis played furiously on his banjo for a few minutes while the band backed him up. The audience cheered. Elvis grinned as he played his banjo; he was in his element. A pair of robins danced in time with the music. Elvis finished his impromptu solo, and then resumed singing.

You ain't nothing but a sea lion, lying on a buoy.
You ain't nothing but a sea lion, lying on a buoy.
Well you ain't never caught a salmon and you ain't no friend of mine.

When they said that you weren't lazy, well that was just a lie.
When they said that you weren't lazy, well that was just a lie.
Well you ain't never caught a salmon and you ain't no friend of mine.

The band abruptly stopped playing and Elvis simultaneously started strumming furiously on his banjo again. His banjo solo caused the audience to break out into a round of applause. The audience members hooted and hollered and stamped their feet in time to the music. Some of the geese in the front row started dancing while Dusty watched in amazement. The band joined in with Elvis again and the beach was once again flooded with music. Elvis winked at a female fur seal who promptly fainted.

"Come on Dusty," shouted Jill above the music. "Let's dance."

"I don't know if I can," responded Dusty. "My body is still kind of sore."

"It will help loosen you up," said Jill as she started to dance.

Dusty started to stiffly dance along with Jill while the audience in the immediate vicinity cheered them on. The audience clapped and stomped.. Dusty's body started to limber up a little and he was having a lot of fun in spite of the fact that he wasn't dancing very well.

A mallard duck was watching Dusty's ungainly movements with bewildered amazement, and said just a little bit too loudly, "I'm telling ya, that pigeon can't dance!"

The music stopped as if a phonograph needle had been dragged across a record. All noise stopped as everyone looked at the duck. The duck nervously looked around and became uncomfortable with the fact that he was now the center of some rather hostile attention. It's usually not a good idea to insult the person to whom the song is dedicated, and the poor duck was quickly figuring that out for himself. As soon as he made that connection, he decided that it was time to leave.

"I think that it is time for me to resume my journey north for the summer," said the duck to no one in particular. "Excuse me, pardon me, coming through," he said as he pushed his way through the crowd. "Excuse me, pardon me, coming through." As soon as he was outside of the audience, he flew away, heading north.

"One, two, a one two three four," said Elvis. The band resumed playing its rock and roll melody. Dusty however, decided not to continue dancing. He had had enough for one day. Elvis continued with his song.

> *You ain't nothing but a sea lion, lying on a buoy.*
> *You ain't nothing but a sea lion, lying on a buoy.*
> *Well you ain't never caught a salmon and you ain't no friend of mine.*

The band played the final notes and ended with a stinger.

"Thank you very much, thank you, thank you and *thank you*," said Elvis as he pointed at a female otter. She of course, fainted. "You're a wonderful audience." The audience cheered and whistled at Elvis. Elvis turned and walked off the stage.

Roy, the stage director, walked up to the front of the stage and said in his booming voice, "Ladies and gentlemen, Elvis has left the building." The audience gave one final cheer and then started to disperse. The band members started to put away their instruments, and Roy walked off the stage with Elvis' banjo, to put it away until the next concert.

Elvis walked up to Dusty and Jill. "Well, how did you like my song?"

"It was just wonderful, Elvis," said Jill. "I still can't believe that you dedicated it to us. Thank you so very much. I will never forget this day."

"You're welcome Jill." Elvis turned and looked over at a young female walrus. "Hey baby." The young walrus fainted with a vocal sigh.

"Do women always faint like that around you?" asked Dusty.

"Usually," responded Elvis. "Sometimes they just go into hysterics and scream. I'm sure I'll get used to it by the time I become famous. I will be famous someday, you know. Someday, the name Elvis, will be a common household name. Someday, everyone will be humming my songs."

Dusty had his doubts about that, but wisely kept his opinion to himself. Roy came running up to them. "Excuse me Elvis, but everybody's packed up and ready to go."

"All right Roy, let's get moving," responded Elvis.

Roy ran off and Elvis turned back to Dusty and Jill. "You two take care now. And if you ever get down to Aqua World, look me up. I just know that they're going to hire me and my band. We'll be famous in no time."

"Goodbye, Elvis," said Dusty and Jill. They watched the band move off down the beach and an eerie silence descended.. Dusty looked around and noticed that most of the audience had already left. It had been a short concert, but it was a lot of fun.

"Good riddance," said a raspy voice behind Dusty.

"And don't come back," added a wheezing voice.

Dusty and Jill spun around.

"Flim!" said Dusty.

"Flam!" said Jill.

"I can hardly hear a thing," said Flim.

"My ears are still ringing," said Flam.

"The music was too loud," said Flim.

"It shook the walls in our cave," said Flam.

"The lyrics were idiotic," said Flim.

"Nonsensical gibberish," said Flam.

"Sea lions everywhere will be insulted," said Flim.

"That could be a good thing, you know," said Flam.

"Well, the music did have a good beat," said Flim.

"Good dance music," said Flam.

"Maybe he'll come back someday," said Flim.

"And insult some more animals," said Flam.

The two old crabs walked off, laughing hysterically, as Dusty and Jill watched in absolute amazement. Dusty wasn't quite sure about what had just happened. They looked at each other and shrugged their shoulders. Who could understand the mind of a hermit crab?

"I will probably never understand those two old crabs," said Dusty.

"That's just as well, Dusty. I would be really worried about you if you did understand them. To understand them, you'd have to be like them. So how did you like the song that Elvis sang?"

Dusty thought about it for a moment. The song was really rather degrading, unless you didn't like sea lions. If you thought that sea lions were fat, lazy animals that did nothing but lay on buoys all day, then the song was fine. He didn't really care at all for Elvis' singing voice, either. He did not understand why women fainted at a mere wink from Elvis. But Elvis could play the banjo very well indeed. And his back-up band was superb.

"Well, I've never heard anyone sing before, so I have nothing to compare him to," said Dusty.

He could tell by the look on Jill's face that his answer was not what she wanted to hear. It was time to change tactics.

"But he really was rather good. I don't think anyone could play a banjo as well as he does. His band was excellent, and he did dedicate his song to us. Not every musician would do that. He really is someone very special."

That turned out to be exactly the right thing to say. Jill simply beamed. Dusty breathed a sigh of relief. She gave Dusty a light peck on the cheek and turned and watched as Elvis and his band disappeared around a bend.

They turned and started up the beach, in the opposite direction that Elvis had taken. They were each silent as they thought about the morning's fun and excitement. Neither one had ever been to a concert

THE SEAGULL WHO WAS AFRAID TO FLY

before or, for that matter, had even heard about one before today. The music and dancing would be something that they would remember for a long time.

They vaguely heard the sound of air rushing through large wings high over their heads. They were too preoccupied with their thoughts to pay any attention to the noise. The quiet sound circled around behind them and faded out.

A small shadow darkened the ground around them and quickly grew larger. They looked down at the shadow with surprise. Then it occurred to then to look up and see what was creating the shadow.

It was too late.

Before they had the chance to look up, a heavy object dropped onto the ground between them and they found themselves being smothered by large wings. Dusty and Jill coughed and sputtered as they fought to catch their breath. They found it very difficult to breathe.

Chapter Six

"Surprised you didn't I! Come on, admit it, you were surprised, *ay*."

Dusty twisted around and looked up to view his captor. He found himself looking at a young Canadian goose. The goose's body was full-grown but its feathers were not completely matured. Neither was the goose. The goose had a rather mischievous twinkle its eyes.

"You're smothering us, you lout!" exclaimed Jill.

"Oh oh, oops—sorry about that, *ay*. Great goose eggs, but am I ever glad to have stumbled across you two," said the goose as he folded his wings onto his back and wiggled his tail feathers.

"Stumbled across?" said Dusty.

"Plowed into, I'd say," responded Jill as she smoothed out her feathers. She was annoyed at the goose for ruffling her feathers. She reached around and started to preen the feathers on her back.

"Yeah, yeah, yeah," said the goose as he admired his tail feathers. "Anyway, what a coincidence it is, running into you two, *ay*."

"Literally, I think," said Dusty.

"Wow what a concert!" continued the goose. "And to think, it was dedicated to you guys, *ay*. Do you guys really know Elvis? Could you introduce me to him sometime? Do you think you could?"

"We don't even know who you are," said Dusty.

"I'm not really sure that I want to," muttered Jill.

"My name is Bryan," said the goose. "I'm a Canadian goose, *ay*."

"Why do you always say the word 'ay'?" asked Dusty.

"Because I'm a Canadian goose, and that's the way Canadians talk, *ay*. So what about it, can you introduce me to Elvis?"

"We don't really know him all that much," said Dusty.

"We just met him yesterday," added Jill.

"Wow, and already you're good friends," said Bryan. "That's really something else. Gosh but I'm hungry, I haven't eaten all day. How about you two? Are you guys hungry?"

Dusty and Jill looked at each other in bewilderment. Bryan was indeed a strange goose. His thoughts seemed to race a thousand miles a minute and in a thousand different directions. But he was right about one thing, and that was that they were hungry.

"Well yes, I am kind of hungry," responded Dusty.

"So am I now that you mention it," said Jill.

"Great," said Bryan, "'cause I'm hungry enough to eat a whole corn field, *ay*. I'm surprised my tummy hasn't started growling yet. My tummy makes a terrible noise when it starts to growl that you don't want to hear. Do you?"

"No!" exclaimed Jill. "We really don't want to hear your tummy rumbles. Thank you anyway."

"Oh okay, I know a really good little restaurant that's just up the beach. Come on, follow me," honked Bryan.

"But. . ." said Dusty, as he waved his right wing at Bryan, trying to get his attention.

Dusty and Jill looked at each other in bewilderment.

"I guess we might as well follow him," said Jill.

Bryan started waddling up the beach with a lumbering gait. Since his legs were longer than those of Dusty and Jill, he was walking much faster than they were. Dusty and Jill had to run in order to keep up with him. It not only tired them out, but it worked up their appetites even more. A few minutes later, they came upon an outdoor café. The café had a sign with the word "Frenchy's" painted on it in big blue letters.

Frenchy's was a quaint little café with tables carved out of driftwood. Old chairs and logs had been neatly placed around the tables. Unlit candles were on each table, which would create a romantic atmosphere in the evenings. Large umbrellas covered each table to keep the sun off the customers during the day. Savory scents and smells wafted through the air, beckoning to the weary travelers.

An old pelican wearing a faded maroon beret was softly playing

French music on an accordion that was very pleasant to listen to.

They entered the café and stood patiently waiting next to a sign that said, "Please wait to be seated." They didn't have long to wait. A French poodle saw them and came over to where they were waiting. He had a large but neatly trimmed mustache that curled up at the ends. He looked very prim and proper.

"Bonjour Monsieurs and Mademoiselle, if you would follow me s'il vous plaît," said the poodle with a very heavy French accent, "I will show you to your table."

They followed the poodle over to their table. He made sure each one was seated and then placed a menu on the table in front of each one of them.

"Can I get you anything to drink?" asked the poodle.

"Some water would be wonderful," said Jill.

"I'd like some water also," said Dusty.

"I'd like some Canada Wet Ginger Ale," said Bryan.

The poodle gave Bryan a disgusted look.

"Very well, two waters and one ginger ale," said the poodle, who promptly departed.

They all opened up their menus and tried to read the selections. The menu was written in French. Unfortunately, none of them could read French. They tried anyway. They didn't have any luck.

The poodle returned with their drinks and set them on the table. He watched them carefully to see if they were ready to order. He was used to giving customers more time to read the menu. Most customers had a difficult time choosing which delicacy they wanted to order. It never occurred to the poodle that the problem was that the menus were written in French, which no one could read.

"French food is usually pretty good," said Bryan. "You know that the French originally came from Canada, don't you?"

The French poodle started shaking and clenched his jaw shut. He disliked serving Canadian geese because he considered them to be rather arrogant and boisterous. On top of that, they almost always left feathers on the floor, and they were sloppy eaters. He tried his best not to look upset. He didn't quite succeed. His mustache twitched.

"No I didn't know that," responded Dusty.

"It's true. That's why the French are such good cooks, they learned their culinary skills from the Canadians, *ay*."

The poodle emitted a quiet but high-pitched noise. This was too much. He was trained to ignore the comments of customers, but he could only ignore so much. The goose was quickly pushing him to his limit. The old pelican stopped playing his accordion and paused to listen.

A family of sea turtles at the next table stopped eating and turned their heads to watch.

"I think you've got that backwards, Bryan," said Jill as she glanced at the poodle. She noticed that the poodle was becoming agitated.

"Well maybe, but look at all these words on the menu," said Bryan, "I can't even read them."

"That is because the words are written in French, you uncivilized goose," said the poodle in a strained voice. "This *is* a French restaurant."

"French restaurant," piped the youngest turtle at the next table.

"Shhh," said the mother turtle.

"Hey waiter, I hope you've got some good grub here, *ay*," honked Bryan.

"Tout au contraire, we do not serve 'grubs' here monsieur, and I am not a waiter. I am the maitre d," said the poodle. He let out a heavy sigh. These customers obviously had no idea how important his job was. His mustache twitched again.

"Grubs!" squeaked the youngest turtle. His mother promptly put more food into his mouth. The oldest daughter giggled. The father sea turtle gave her a stern glace.

"If you don't serve grubs, do you serve geese?" asked Bryan with a chuckle.

The poodle rolled his eyes and made an irritated sound. He had obviously heard that joke before and he was not impressed. This was clearly not going to be a good day for him. He took a moment and regained his composure. He smoothed out his mustache.

"I suppose that was an attempt at humor, monsieur. A very poor attempt, I might add. We only serve geese when they are in season," responded the poodle without a smile. "But I'll make an exception in your case."

"I want to eat goose," exclaimed the youngest turtle. The oldest daughter tried hard not to laugh, and almost succeeded. Unfortunately, her mouth was full of milk, which sprayed out when she could no longer contain her laughter. The father sea turtle found himself covered with milk. Mama sea turtle quickly handed him a napkin.

Bryan swallowed hard (which is an impressive sight considering the length of a goose's neck) and shook his head. He wasn't sure whether or not the poodle was joking. "No thank you, I think I'll pass," he said.

"What is a maitre d?" asked Dusty.

"The maitre d is the person in charge of the customers," responded the poodle. "I am the headwaiter. It is a tremendous responsibility and I take my job very seriously."

"We are very honored that you are personally serving us," said Jill.

"Thank you Mademoiselle," said the poodle to Jill. He was pleased that at least the two seagulls appeared to be civilized. "With what can we tempt your taste buds today?"

"Please," said Jill, "call me Jill. "I don't know what to eat; everything on the menu looks delicious. What do you recommend?" She didn't want to admit that she couldn't read the French words on the menu.

"Very well, Jill," said the poodle, "you may call me François. I am here to serve. I recommend the seaweed sautéed in butter with sea onions, served on top of a bed of deep fat fried kelp. All of our ingredients are, of course, gathered daily so you may be assured of their quality and freshness."

"Oh that sounds delicious, François," said Jill. "I'll take a plate of that."

"Me too," said Dusty.

"That's what I'll eat, too," said Bryan. "But I got to know, Francis, is that kelp fried in animal or vegetable fat?"

François turned bright red as he tried hard not to explode. His mustache uncurled and straightened out flat all by itself. French poodles are an easily excitable breed and François was no exception. François fought down the urge to run around in small little circles yapping furiously. This of course, took a lot of effort for the poodle. But such behavior would have been undignified, so he suppressed the urge. Dusty thought he saw wisps of smoke coming out of François' ears.

"My name is 'François,' not 'Francis,' and we normally use goose fat," said François very slowly as he tried to control his temper. "We're almost out and we need more." At this point François lost control of his temper, which is also not unusual for small dogs.

"Of course we use vegetable fat, you stupid goose!" he exploded. "I am French, not barbarian!" François turned and stomped off toward the kitchen muttering words in French that no one understood. The old pelican resumed playing his accordion.

"Is the goose a barbeon?" asked the youngest turtle.

"Barbarian dear, yes, now eat your food," responded the mother turtle. Everyone in the sea turtle family looked at the oldest daughter to make sure she wasn't going spray food in their direction. The oldest daughter pulled her head down inside her shell. They all heard the sound of muffled laughter coming out of her shell. The sea turtle family tried very hard to hide their grins.

"That wasn't very nice, Bryan," said Jill.

"I think you made him very upset," added Dusty.

"Oh well," said Bryan, "you know how French poodles are—no sense of humor, *ay*. So tell me Dusty, how did you guys meet Elvis?"

"It was an accident," responded Dusty who was surprised by Bryan's abrupt change of subject.

"Isn't that how everyone meets, by accident?" asked Bryan.

"No, he means it was because of an accident that we met Elvis," responded Jill.

"Oh," said Bryan who very clearly did not understand.

"I flew into a log and knocked myself unconscious," said Dusty. "Elvis saw me crash and came over to help."

"And that's how we met Elvis," said Jill.

"Why did you crash into a log?" asked Bryan with a puzzled look on his face.

"It was my first attempt at flying and I didn't know how to stop," said Dusty.

"I don't think that I would recommend using a log to stop myself," said Bryan. "That would certainly put a crick in my neck. But I suppose that's one way to do it ay. But I'm curious: you said it was your first time to fly. Why haven't you flown before now?"

"I'm afraid of heights," responded Dusty. "The trouble with flying is that you have to look down. I don't like to look down because I get sick."

"Wow, that is definitely a problem, *ay*," said Bryan.

"I tried a low level flight yesterday and ended up crashing into a log," said Dusty. "I don't want to repeat that experience again."

"So what about you Bryan," said Jill. "What are you doing here?"

"Oh, well, I was flying north for the summer with the flock, *ay*," said Bryan, "when I saw them setting up for the concert. So I dropped out of formation and flew down to catch the show. What a pleasant surprise I got when I found out it was Elvis."

"You've heard of Elvis before today?" asked Dusty.

"Of course," said Bryan, "everybody's heard of Elvis."

"Are you allowed to drop out of flying formation?" asked Jill.

"Well no, but I did it anyway," said Bryan. "After all, I'm not an adult, so I don't have to behave responsibly, *ay*."

"That's not true, Dusty," said Jill, "don't believe him. You should always be responsible and ask permission. Right Bryan?"

Bryan sheepishly hung his head, which can be a long way for a goose. "I suppose you're right," he replied.

"Of course I'm right," said Jill.

"Will you get in trouble?" asked Dusty.

"Probably," said Bryan, "but I seem to be in trouble quite a bit anyway."

"I'm not surprised," said Jill. "Oh look, here comes our food."

François brought out three plates of steaming food which he then placed in front of them. He made sure that everyone had napkins before he turned to leave.

"Bon appétit, enjoy your meal," said François.

THE SEAGULL WHO WAS AFRAID TO FLY

They tied the napkins around their necks (a neat trick if you're a goose) and then started eating. The food was so tasty that even Bryan stopped talking in order to eat. François checked on them several times, but they were so busy eating that they barely even noticed him. When they were finally finished eating, he came to clear away their plates.

"This seaweed dish was wonderful, François," said Jill.

"Thank you, Mademoiselle," said François. "It is always a pleasure to serve a beautiful creature such as yourself."

Jill blushed.

"I didn't know it was possible to make seaweed taste so good," said Dusty. "I think that this was the best meal I've ever eaten."

"Thank you, Monsieur," said Francois. "Here at Frenchy's, we strive to make the ordinary into a feast for the taste buds. We take great pride in our culinary skills." He glared at Bryan for a moment then turned again to speak to Dusty. "It was a pleasure to serve you."

"Well Franzwhat, I've got admit that you serve the best food this side of Canada, *ay*," said Bryan.

"My name is 'François,' and we serve the best food anywhere," said François, who was becoming extremely annoyed with the impertinent goose.

"Tell you what," said Bryan, "I'll just call you Frank to avoid confusion, *ay*."

"Are you mocking me?" asked a very red-faced François.

"Oh no," said Bryan, "I'm a goose, not a mocking bird; therefore, I don't mock."

"Mocking goose!" blurted the youngest turtle.

"Come along, dear," said the mother turtle, "it's time for us leave." The turtle family got up from the table and left the café.

Bryan started to laugh at the cleverness of his play on words. Most of the time, just hearing a goose laugh is enough to make most animals smile. Honking laughter will do that to you. François, however, was not smiling. He was not amused. He was angry. Suddenly François started yapping furiously and charged straight at Bryan.

Bryan's eyes opened wide with surprise and with a startled honk, he ran out of the café with François right on his tail feathers. As soon as he was out of the café, Bryan flapped his wings and flew up into the air. He practically bowled over the sea turtle family. They all ducked their heads into their shells. As it was, he just barely missed them. He quickly headed north to catch up with his flock.

"Good riddance, au revoir, so long, and don't come back!" shouted François as he shook his paw at the fleeing goose.

François smoothed out his mustache and made sure it was properly curled. He nodded to the sea turtle family who had popped their heads back up and were staring at him in astonishment. As soon as he was sure that he was presentable, he reentered the café. He walked up to Dusty and Jill and gave them a wink.

"I must apologize for my behavior, but that certainly felt good," said François.

"No apology is necessary, François," said Jill. "I think you did us a favor."

"Did you see the size of Bryan's eyes?" giggled Dusty. "I thought they were going to explode."

"There is nothing worse than a rude customer," said François. But then he grinned. "His eyes did become the size of pancakes didn't they?" He chuckled to himself and headed off to the kitchen.

"Come on Jill, it's time for us to be on our way as well," said Dusty.

They walked over to the base of the ledge and resumed their journey. Since this portion of the ledge was steep, careful attention to their walking was required. It took them a while to walk up the steep section, but the ledge began to level off and walking became much easier. By early evening they squeezed past the pile of rocks. Their walking slowed as they became increasingly tired. Their walking then slowed to trudging, and then stopped altogether.

"I never thought that I would be walking back up this ledge," panted Dusty.

"I've never done this much walking before," said Jill. "I don't know how you managed to walk all this way and still have webbing on your feet. I think I need a new pair of feet."

"I didn't walk as much in one day as we just did. It took me three days the first time I walked this ledge. Do you see that plant just up ahead? That's where I spent my first night. If we can just walk that far, it would be a good place for us to stop tonight."

"That's a long walk, but it would be a good place to spend the night," said Jill.

After several hours of walking, they slowly shuffled their way up to the plant. They both worked their way behind the plant and curled up next to each other. They were both asleep before they could even say good night to each other. Their exhausted bodies quickly took them into a very deep slumber. They slept until noon the next day.

When they awoke they were surprised to see the sun so high up in the sky. They stretched and yawned and checked to make sure they had worn no holes in their feet. They resumed walking and soon came to where the nest used to be located. Dusty looked at the area with a lump in his throat. Memories came flooding back to him.

"This is where the nest used to be," said Dusty. "A lot has happened to me since I left here."

"You're not the same seagull that you were the day you left. You've grown a lot. You've matured a lot. You're a better seagull because of what you've experienced. Come on, lets keep going."

"I suppose you're right, we really should move on," agreed Dusty.

Jill urged him on. They soon came to a place where about ten feet of the ledge had crumbled away. Dusty looked at it in despair, wondering how he was going to get across that precipice.

"The only way across is to fly, Dusty," said Jill.

"Fly?" said Dusty hysterically. "I have to fly across that?"

"I don't know any other way."

"Oh no," said Dusty in despair.

"I'm sorry Dusty," said Jill, "but I just don't know of any other way to do this. I wish I could think of a way, but I can't."

"Then I'm just going to do it," said Dusty with determination, "before I talk myself out of it."

"No, Dusty, wait!" cried Jill.

But it was too late. Dusty nervously spread his wings, and walked to edge of the ledge. The updraft caught him before he knew what was happening. His nervousness transformed into fear as the current of air rushing upward caught his wings and lifted him up. His body shot straight up into the air. His eyes were frozen open in terror as he watched the rock wall of the bluff rushed past him in a blur of earthen colors.

"Jill!" screamed Dusty. "Jill, help me!"

Chapter Seven

Jill spread her wings and let the updraft lift her off the ledge. She flapped her wings as hard as she could and flew after Dusty. She quickly caught up with him since he wasn't trying to fly. They both reached the top of the bluff simultaneously.

"Dusty," said Jill, "turn to the right."

"How?" asked Dusty.

"Lower your right wing and raise your left wing."

Dusty followed Jill's instructions and curved off to the right. He glided away from the edge of the bluff and the treacherous updraft of air, which had flung him upwards. He saw that Jill was flying right beside him.

"Ok Dusty, that was good, you can straighten out now," said Jill. "Now I want you to back-flap your wings to stop your forward momentum."

Dusty back-flapped his wings and he came to a stop. He was now hovering about twelve feet above the ground. He looked down at the ground below him and quickly looked back at Jill.

"What now?" asked Dusty.

"We're going to glide down now," responded Jill. "Stop flapping and set your wings out straight." Dusty did as he was instructed. "Good, now tilt your wings down and forward just a little bit. That's perfect Dusty! You see how we're slowly going forward but descending at the same time?"

Dusty nodded his head. He wasn't sure if he wanted this landing to go a little more quickly or a little slower. He simply wanted to be back on solid ground. The sooner he got there, the better.

"Watch the ground now," said Jill. "When you get about two feet above the ground, back-flap your wings and let yourself slowly settle to the ground. Okay, get ready, here we go."

Dusty back-flapped his wings and plopped down onto the ground. He landed with a little more speed and a lot harder than he would have preferred, but at least he was down on the ground again. This time, he landed without knocking himself unconscious.

"That was a great landing, Dusty!" said Jill. "You see, you're getting better all the time. You didn't even look like you were afraid."

"Are you kidding?" responded Dusty. "I was too afraid to be afraid. I mean, I was scared silly."

"That's a double negative," croaked a voice behind them.

Dusty and Jill whirled around and found themselves looking at a rather large toad. He was brown and green in color and covered with warts. He had small eyes and a large mouth. He had short front legs and extremely long and muscular back legs.

"Too afraid to be afraid is a double negative," continued the toad. "You're not using grammar correctly when you talk that way. Either you are afraid, or you are not. You can't be both. That doesn't really matter, however. What matters is the fact that you," the toad pointed at Dusty, "landed on my lunch."

Dusty looked down at his feet and took a couple of steps backwards. He had landed on top of a dandelion. A large horsefly had been sitting on the dandelion. Dusty had squashed them both when he landed. Dusty wasn't quite sure what to say to the toad.

"I'm very sorry Mr. Toad," said Dusty.

"Mr. Toad?" the toad shook head and sighed. "Toads just don't get any respect. My name is Phred. That's spelled P-H-R-E-D, Phred. Not Mr. Toad."

"Hello Phred, I'm Dusty, and this is Jill."

"It's a pleasure to meet you," said Jill.

"That's an odd way to spell the name, Fred," said Dusty.

"Not to an educated toad like myself," said Phred.

"Oh," said Dusty in awe, "you're a scholar."

"Yes indeed," said Phred. "I graduated from Toad Stool School of

Higher Learning. I earned a degree in Insectum Studium, and in case you don't know what that is, it's the study of insects."

"I have never had the honor of meeting a wise and educated person such as yourself," said Dusty.

"What do you do with the insects that you study?" asked Jill.

"Most of the time I eat them, when I'm finished with my studies, that is. Well, at least you two are polite," said Phred, "even if you did kill my lunch. Most seagulls are ill-mannered, disrespectful, and obnoxious. I don't often see very many seagulls up here, not that I mind, of course. I imagine that's because of the cat."

"Cat?" said Jill.

"What's a cat?" asked Dusty.

"The cat is a big orange furred monster with evil eyes, sharp teeth and deadly claws. They're silent for the most part, sneaking around looking for a meal. They eat seagulls, you know. It tried to eat me once, but it didn't like how I tasted, so now it leaves me alone. But you two had better be careful. The cat loves to catch birds."

"Where does the cat live?" asked Jill.

"You see that lighthouse over there?" said Phred. "That is where the cat resides. The humans who live in the lighthouse feed the cat. The cat simply kills for fun, and for sport. I think it enjoys the thrill of the hunt."

"I don't think I like the sound of that," said Dusty.

"As long as the cat does not know that you are here, you're safe," said Phred. "Just how long are you two planning on staying?"

"Only as long as it takes Dusty to get over his fear of heights," said Jill.

"Oh, so you're afraid of heights, are you?" said Phred to Dusty. Dusty nodded his head. "You have what we scholars refer to as, acrophobia, the fear of heights. Don't be afraid of heights; be afraid of the cat. Heights can't kill you, because you're a bird. The cat will try to kill you, *because* you're a bird. Now if you don't mind, I must bid you adieu. That's French for goodbye."

The toad hopped away with great leaps from his powerful legs. In a minute, he was completely out of sight. Dusty continued to stare long after Phred was out of sight. Jill's voice broke Dusty out of his trance.

"What a remarkable creature," said Jill.

"Yes he was," said Dusty as he turned to look at Jill.

"We might as well put Paco's plan into action, since we're up here," said Jill.

"I guess so, but we'll have to be on the lookout for that cat," said Dusty.

Dusty and Jill turned and started walking toward the bluff. The grass that they were walking on gave way to rock as they came close to the edge. Dusty could feel his nervousness returning as they neared the edge. The thought of looking over the edge did not exactly thrill him. They heard the lonely sound of the wind as it rushed up the side of the cliff. Dusty wisely decided to keep his wings folded in close to his body.

"Ok Dusty, this is it," said Jill. "Take a quick peek over the edge."

Dusty swallowed nervously and cautiously poked his head over the side. He could feel the rush of air as it blew past his face and had to squint his eyes to adjust for it. He looked down. The ocean lay far below him. It was an awfully long drop. He pulled his head back over the edge and sat down. He then realized that he had been holding his breath. He slowly let it out.

"Well?" asked Jill.

"I don't feel sick or woozy, but I certainly don't like looking down."

"The important thing is that you didn't get sick. The next time you look down, we'll increase the amount of time, just like Paco told us. You're doing great, Dusty. What do you say we find ourselves some dinner?"

"That sounds good to me," said Dusty. "What do you have in mind?"

"There are some dandelions in that clump of weeds right over there," said Jill as she pointed along the edge. "Dandelion greens are tender and tasty, and I'm hungry."

They walked together along the edge of the bluff and soon came to the clump of weeds. They pulled the greens off the dandelions and ate until they were full. Dusty had no idea that a dandelion could be used for food, as long as he didn't eat the yellow center of the weed. They were about to leave when they were suddenly interrupted by a small quiet and shy voice.

"Excuse me," said the tiny voice, "but could you spare some those dandelion greens?"

Dusty and Jill looked down and saw a small female shrew looking up at them. She had short gray fur, long whiskers, and small dark eyes. She was wearing an apron and kept wringing her hands as she nervously looked around.

"Yes, we'll get you some dandelion greens," said Jill, "it would be my pleasure."

Jill started pulling the small tender leaves off some dandelions and laid them down by the shrew. Dusty forgot to help because he was gawking at the shrew. He had forgotten that it is not polite to stare. The little shrew picked up the dandelion greens and stuffed them into the pockets on her apron.

"Thank you very much," said the shrew. "My children will eat well tonight."

"You're welcome," said Jill. "My name is Jill. My friend with his mouth hanging open is Dusty."

Dusty promptly closed his mouth.

"My name is Mrs. Weatherby," said the shrew, "but everyone calls me Penny."

"Why does everyone call you Penny?" asked Dusty.

"It's my name," responded Penny.

"Oh," said Dusty who felt rather foolish.

"It's a pleasure to meet you Penny," said Jill.

"It's a pleasure to meet you also," said Penny.

"Do all shrews wear aprons?" asked Dusty.

"Oh no," said Penny, "I just wear this when I gather food, or when I clean the house. You see, it's much easier to gather food when I can put it in the pockets of my apron. I can also gather more food this way. And I don't have to gather food as often. It's safer if you don't have to go out very much. It can be very dangerous outside." The shrew anxiously glanced around.

"Why is it dangerous to be outside?" asked Dusty.

"The cat," whispered Penny as she looked around again. "We have to be very careful of the cat. It likes to eat mice and shrews. You have to be very cautious, or the cat will get you."

"What can you tell us about this cat?" asked Jill.

"It's the largest, most hideous creature I've ever seen," said Penny. "It has fangs that are as big as my body, and claws that can shred a tree. It has long orange fur and moves as quietly as the night itself. It is a horror to behold. I know, because I saw it once, and managed to live to tell about it."

"What happened?" asked Dusty.

"I was out gathering food that day, with my apron, and I was on my way back home. I was almost to the hole when I smelled something foul. It was a scent that I was unfamiliar with. So I stopped and sniffed the air. I knew that something was wrong because everything had become quiet. Even the crickets were silent. It made me very nervous.

"I moved with quietness and stealth. I crept closer and closer to the hole leading down to my house. The hole was in sight when suddenly I thought I saw its tail above the grass for a moment. I stood stock-still and remained motionless. I then slowly looked around, sniffing the air. That's when I saw it! It saw me at the same time and it crouched down to prepare itself to pounce. But I didn't wait. I ran as fast as I could for the hole. I just barely made it in time. The cat pounced and tore at the hole behind me with its claws. But I was safe in the hole. I scampered down the tunnel to my house, but it took me awhile to catch my breath. I was a nervous wreck for days. But now I'm extremely cautious, and you should be, too. I have been out far too long now, and must go home."

The little shrew scampered away with her dandelion greens.

"Good-bye Mrs. Weatherby," waved Jill. The shrew turned around, waved, and then disappeared into the ground.

"We seem to meet the most interesting creatures," said Dusty.

"Yes we do," laughed Jill, "but that's what makes life so interesting. You never know whom you'll meet next. Come on, it's time for you to look over the edge again."

"Already?" asked Dusty.

THE SEAGULL WHO WAS AFRAID TO FLY

"There's no time like the present," responded Jill.

"Okay, let's get this over with," said Dusty as he headed for the edge. Jill laughed and walked beside him.

"This time, don't hold your breath," said Jill. "Breathe and relax; it's not like you're going to fall over the edge."

"You had to say that, didn't you?" said Dusty. Jill laughed.

Dusty managed to look over the edge while Jill counted out loud to ten. He still held his breath but he didn't mention that to Jill. He thought she might want him to do it again if she knew. The important thing in Dusty's mind was that he did not get dizzy while he was looking down.

They spent the rest of the evening exploring the area. They kept some distance between themselves and the lighthouse because they thought the cat might be nearby. Late that afternoon, they started to get hungry again. They had seen no sign of the cat, but they remained cautious and alert.

"Let's go over to those blueberry bushes to get something to eat," said Jill.

"I've never eaten blueberries," said Dusty.

"You'll love them, they're so sweet and juicy," responded Jill.

They wandered into a field until they came to the blueberry bushes that Jill had seen earlier. They pulled the berries off the bushes and ate until they were full. The berries not only satisfied their appetite, but also quenched their thirst at the same time. Dusty's beak and face were covered with berry juice.

"Your beak and face are all blue," laughed Jill.

Dusty stuck his tongue out at her, which was also quite blue. Jill doubled over in laughter. She stuck out her tongue so Dusty could see what it looked like. Jill's tongue was also blue. Dusty started laughing also. Jill licked the end of her wing and cleaned the blueberry juice off of Dusty's face and beak. They continued walking until they came back to the bluff and soon found their way blocked by bramble bushes.

"It looks like we could slip under these bushes and spend the night here," said Dusty. "I don't think that cat could get us in there."

"That's a good idea," said Jill. "But we'll have to be careful, those thorns look really sharp. I don't like the idea of getting poked by them."

They squatted down and then carefully and cautiously worked their way in under the bushes. They quickly came to a small clearing, which had plenty of space for the two seagulls to stand up. It was the perfect place to spend the night. They sat down, snuggled up against each other, and drifted off to sleep.

Late that night, the cat walked up to the bramble bushes as it was making its rounds. It sniffed the ground and could smell that a bird or two was hiding in the bush. But the cat could not get underneath the bramble bushes to where Dusty and Jill were hiding. The cat watched the bushes for several minutes, but saw that nothing was moving. It silently vanished back into the night.

The bright sun rose into a cloudless, windless sky. The sea was almost completely flat and smooth. From the top of the bluff, you could see forever. The sun slowly warmed the ground as insects and small animals came out to drink the dew off the leaves upon which it had settled. Dusty and Jill crawled out from the bramble bushes and yawned. They stretched their wings and legs and looked with pleasure at the beautiful day.

"Blueberries for breakfast?" asked Dusty.

"Sounds okay to me," responded Jill.

They walked back out to the field where the blueberry bushes were located. As they were eating, Dusty slowly moved about two feet away from Jill. He waited until he saw that she wasn't looking in his direction. He picked up a blueberry and threw it at her. It narrowly missed her head. Jill looked over at Dusty who was eating a blueberry with a very innocent look on his face. A blueberry hit Dusty square on the right wing. Suddenly, blueberries were flying everywhere. Dusty and Jill threw blueberries and laughed until they collapsed on the ground. Dusty brushed the blueberries off his body and noticed that Jill had not even one blueberry mark on her body. Every blueberry that he had thrown had missed. That caused both of them to go into another fit of laughter.

The noise of their laughter drifted over to the lighthouse and caught the attention of the cat. It slowly and carefully started walking into the field toward the blueberry bushes. It paused every so often to listen to the ruckus being raised by the two seagulls. When Dusty and Jill's laughter died down, the cat stopped moving, but its tail twitched in anticipation. It was very close to the blueberry bushes.

"Come on Dusty," laughed Jill, "we have got to get you cleaned up."

"Oh okay," responded Dusty.

They started walking back toward the bluff. Jill thought she might find some leaves on the bigger plants with enough dew on them to clean Dusty with. The cat raised its head and watched Dusty and Jill walk away. It followed them at a discrete distance. Jill eventually found some plants with large leaves that were covered with dew.

"Alright Dusty," said Jill, "wash yourself with these leaves. I'm going to take a look to see if the dew made any puddles on the rocks. Maybe I can find one with enough water in it to give you a bath. I don't think I'll find anything, but it never hurts to look. Oh and Dusty, wash behind your ears."

Jill headed off toward the bluff while Dusty started washing himself with the leaves. By the time he was finished, he was amazed at how clean he was. Almost all of the blueberry stains had washed off. He was sure that Jill would be pleased. He stood up and looked around. He didn't see Jill anywhere.

Dusty rubbed one last leaf behind his ears and started walking toward the bluff in the direction that Jill had gone. He didn't feel the necessity to call out Jill's name because he was sure he would see her when he came to the rocks. He popped out of the grass and looked around. He saw Jill standing with her back to him about fifty yards away. He decided it would be fun to sneak up on her. He obviously hadn't learned anything from the results of the blueberry fight.

Jill was standing near the edge of the bluff looking out at the ocean. She was singing a pretty song to herself and never noticed Dusty sneaking along the grass line. Dusty was walking slowly, trying not to make any noise, and was actually being rather successful in his attempt at stealth. He was enjoying himself immensely and stopped moving when another movement caught his attention. He peered at the grass for a moment to see what had moved. That was when he saw the cat.

The cat was concentrating on Jill and hadn't even noticed Dusty, probably because Dusty had also been sneaking up on Jill. The cat was only about five yards away from Jill, and Dusty was about five yards away from the cat. Dusty wasn't sure just what he should do. The cat crouched down and became difficult for Dusty to see. Dusty remembered the words of the shrew and realized that the cat was preparing itself to pounce.

The thought that the cat was going to try to kill Jill filled Dusty with rage. He lowered his head and charged at the cat. Dusty had already shown an aptitude for acting without thinking, so it is really no surprise that he ran straight at the cat. It certainly surprised the cat.

"Jill," screamed Dusty. "Jill, fly away! Fly away Jill! The cat is here! Get away now!"

Jill turned around and looked at Dusty. Then she saw what Dusty was doing. She rose up into the air and started to circle around. The cat heard Dusty calling out and turned its head to look at Dusty. Perhaps it had never seen a seagull going berserk. Perhaps the cat had never had a bird run straight at it before. Whatever the reason, the cat was too surprised to move. That is until Dusty ran right into it.

The cat yowled in pain and jumped straight up into the air. Dusty tumbled head over heels and ended up on the rock near the edge of the bluff. Dusty stood up, shook himself off, and looked around for the cat. He was having a hard time believing that he had just run into the cat.

The cat had run about ten yards away from Dusty and stood there hissing. The cat was very obviously upset. The cat bared its teeth and flexed its claws. Dusty started to back away from the cat. The cat screamed its defiance and rushed at Dusty. Dusty turned and fled.

Unfortunately, Dusty did not pay attention to which direction he ran. Years later he would claim that instinct took over. Perhaps it was fate. In either case, Dusty ran right over the edge of the Bluff. He was extremely surprised at his action. So was the cat.

Dusty instinctively spread his wings and soared away from the bluff. The cat came skidding to a stop just inches away from the edge, and just moments away from actually catching Dusty. Dusty circled around and watched the cat skid to a stop. Dusty was safe, and he looked around for Jill and saw her flying up beside him.

"Dusty! You were fantastic! You just saved my life. And look at you, you're flying! You're actually flying!"

"I guess I had to have the fear frightened out of me," responded Dusty. "I can even look down! This is amazing!"

"I knew you could do it," said Jill, "I always knew that you would. Let's fly over to Paco's buoy and tell him the good news."

"That's a great idea!" responded Dusty.

"You were wonderful with that cat," said Jill. "Did you see how high it jumped? I'll bet it thinks twice before it tries to catch a seagull again. You are a hero, Dusty."

"Oh shucks," stammered Dusty.

"You're going to make a wonderful father someday. Our children are going to turn out just fine with you as their dad."

"Jill?" said Dusty after a moment. "What do you mean Jill? Jill? Jill! Wait up! I have a question."

Phred, the scholarly toad, watched the two seagulls fly off into the distance and chuckled to himself. Dusty still had a lot to learn. In fact, he had a whole lot to learn. He knew that Dusty would somehow survive. He chuckled to himself again as he eyed another horsefly. He could still hear Dusty calling after Jill in the distance.